A SEA CRUISE

*turns into a dangerous adventure
when the Bradys overhear plans for
a robbery.*

Peter and Jan are trapped by crooks
in a cabin, and their lives are
threatened.

The Bradys pursue a band of
jewel thieves through a giant
ship.

*Those are only some of the exciting
adventures you'll find in this book
when you travel with the Bradys
on their "Adventure on the High
Seas."*

THE BRADY BUNCH

in

Adventure on the High Seas

by JACK MATCHA

AN OFFICIAL TIGER BEAT PUBLICATION

Chapter ONE

≋≋≋≋≋≋≋≋≋≋

The idea of sailing into pirate waters on a great ship alive with excitement and color, with salt spray stinging their faces, thrilled the Brady Bunch when their father described it to them. They had no idea, however, that they would also mix with seedy crooks and rough, dangerous characters who would put them in great peril. Had they ever dreamed of all that would happen once they were on the high seas, they might never have left home.

The waterborne adventure began one spring Sunday when Mike Brady took them all to see the enormous steamship, the *Queen Mary* in Long Beach. And that nearly never happened either. When Mike mentioned it, they all hated the idea. Greg, for one, was itching to go surfing instead.

"Me too," Peter cried. "I've been waiting all week."

"I want to go swimming," Marcia added. Before another moment had passed Cindy, Bobby, Jan, all voted for the beach too.

Mike shook his head. "Okay, okay, the beach it is. I just asked, that's all. I just imagined that for a change today you might enjoy seeing all the engines that make the ship move across the ocean, the sea museum, and then wind up with a good lunch in the ship's restaurant."

For a long moment there was silence as the children looked at one another. Then Bobby spoke up softly. "I'd like to see it, Dad. I mean if you really want to go."

"Me too," said Jan. She looked awkwardly at Greg as if she had dealt him a blow. He threw up his hands and sighed. "Oh heck. I can go surfing next week. I'm willing to go, too."

"Oh no," Mike Brady said. "I don't want to force anyone. We can skip it if you really want the beach." He looked into his plate. "After all, it's just a ship almost as big as the Empire State Building, the tallest building in the world. And it carried thousands of soldiers to Europe during World War II. Outside of that it's just a big floating hotel with loads of different rooms, swimming pools, theaters, gymnasiums. All of it on a hull as big as a football field. It might bore you to death."

"As big as a football field?" Peter said, amazed. "I never heard of anything that big on the ocean. Hey, I want to see that, Dad."

"Me too, me too!" Cindy said, jumping up and down. She turned to Greg and Marcia. "Oh please Greg, Marcia tell him you really want to go."

"I do!" Greg said enthusiastically. "Don't you, Marcia?"

"Of course I do," she declared.

6

Mike smiled and pulled several tickets from his pocket. "Well, in that case let's make a beeline for the car. I got these tickets from a friend in the office Friday. It's getting late."

"Hey that's not fair," Alice protested as she served them some more of her delicious pancakes. "What's the idea of fooling us like that? I almost lost my appetite because I thought we weren't going to the ship. I've been dying to see it since it opened to the public."

"Oh, you know Mike," Carol laughed. "He's a big tease."

"Did you know, Mom?" Jan asked grinning.

"No," Carol said. "He had me fooled too. And I've lived with him for years."

"Okay, enough of this chatter," Mike said firmly. "If we don't get started right away, we'll miss lunch on board."

Everybody was in the car in ten minutes.

An hour later they were walking up the gangplank of the most gigantic ship they had ever seen. The ship seemed to go on forever. Indeed, as they entered Long Beach it seemed to make the buildings around it look small by comparison.

The next two hours were like magic to them all. They moved along the enormous decks with their mouths open, examining all the many different types of rooms. Jan and Cindy had to be kept from running up and down the many stairways that led to the other decks.

For Greg and Peter the mammoth engines that powered the ship were the best feature of all. They seemed like toys designed by giants for their own amusement. They could not get close enough or study them enough.

"Wow," Peter said at one point. "Do you realize how much fuel those things eat up. Mountains of oil, I'll bet."

"They probably needed a whole army of guys to keep them going," Greg added as his eyes roamed the metal monsters.

The girls loved the seagoing museum best and the huge dining rooms with their gorgeous decorations.

"It's like some fabulous palace," Marcia whispered as they entered one of them. "Imagine the kind of fantastic meals they served in this place."

"Speaking of meals," Mike said, "It's about time for us to have one. Anybody hungry?"

Everybody yelled yes at once. Mike laughed and led them to a beautiful restaurant that overlooked the blue ocean. They sat near the window and stared as a waiter served them the most delicious food they had ever eaten. Mike let them pick whatever they wanted for the occasion.

"Like it, Peter?" he asked as his son wolfed down an extra helping of pie and ice cream.

"Boy, do I," Peter yelled. "I bet there isn't a restaurant on land that has as many dishes on its menu as this place. Right, Dad?"

"I don't think so, Peter," Mike said. "But this menu's nothing compared to what you have on a ship that's actually going someplace. You see, people get hungry in that brisk sea air and they're starving by the time meals are served. To keep them happy the chefs give them a mountain of food. And all those shipboard games like shuffleboard and deck tennis and swimming in saltwater outdoor pools drives their appetites way up.

"Why I can remember one ocean trip I took where they had over a hundred things on the dinner and lunch and breakfast menus."

"Over a hundred?" cried Cindy. "And you ate them all?"

"I couldn't," laughed her father. "But you can bet I darn near tried. That was the most exciting sea voyage I ever took. Right into the old pirate seas near Jamaica where Captain Kidd and old Morgan and the Spanish silver and gold treasure ships used to sail hundreds of years ago."

"Gee, I'd give anything to make such a trip," Peter sighed.

"So would I," Jan said.

"Would you really?" Mike asked very casually as he put a piece of pineapple pie into his mouth.

"Oh yes," Marcia cried. "Do you think we might, Dad, some day. I mean really sail on a big beautiful ship like this one."

"Well, we might," Mike said cautiously. "If you really wanted to."

"When, when!" Bobby cried excitedly.

"Well, actually I was thinking maybe we might do it in a couple of weeks. I thought we'd possibly take a vacation on a ship this time instead of taking our usual trip to the mountains. But only if you all agreed it was a good idea. I don't want to make you do it otherwise. And of course if your mother agrees. Can't do it without her. And Alice too, of course."

"Oh Mom," Marcia cried. "You want to go, don't you? Please say yes. Please."

In a moment everyone was begging her to agree. Carol smiled and shook her fist at her husband.

"Oh Mike! That's nasty putting it all on me. You know I'm dying to go. I've never taken a cruise like that. But can we really afford it? I mean it'll cost us a fortune to take nine people, won't it?"

"Not really," Mike said. "One of my clients owns a ship line. He offered me a deal. I do his plans for a new building at a low cost and he'll give me a heavy discount. It'll only cost a fraction of what it normally would. If we really want to go, that is. So it's up to you all. How do you feel about it?"

"I'm already packed," Alice said. "Ship ahoy mates!"

Everyone spoke up at the same time to assure him they wanted to go. The table rang with so many excited voices that people around them stared with astonishment.

"Good. Then we're all set," Mike said with satisfaction in his voice. He paused and, with a teasing look in his eyes, smiled across the table.

"That was really why I brought you all down to the *Queen Mary* today, you know. I wanted to give you a taste of shipboard life and see if you could stand for some more."

10

"Oh you son of a gun," Carol said with mock anger. "I ought to toss that roll at you!" She lifted it from the white tablecloth as if she were set to throw it at him.

"Better be nice to me now," Mike said, grinning. "Or I may change my mind."

"Oh, no!" the children all yelled.

"You wouldn't dare after that buildup," Carol cried.

"No, of course I wouldn't," Mike said. "But we've got a lot to do. I want you all to get special shots from the doctor, before the end of the week. Probably won't need them but we'll be stopping at islands where the water might be poor, so there's no use taking chances."

"I'll make appointments for us all with the doctor first thing tomorrow morning," Carol promised. "Let me see, what else do we need for the trip?"

"Clothes, Mom!" Marcia cried. "I'll need all kinds of dresses, sports outfits, shoes . . . everything."

"Me too!" cried Jan. All at once everybody remembered that they had to stock up on new clothes. Greg wanted a new sports jacket, water fins, a fishing pole in case they went fishing off the boat, and goggles for underwater swimming.

Peter wanted new white duck pants for shipboard and Cindy wanted some new playclothes. Naturally Jan, Bobby, and Carol thought of many things they needed too. Alice said she had to take awhile every day to shop for herself.

"Hey, wait a minute, folks," Mike protested.

11

"We're only going off for two weeks and we aren't headed for the moon. You don't need all that, for heaven's sake."

But it was no use trying to argue with them. The idea of going on a sea cruise had seized all their imaginations and they could not stop talking about all the things they had to buy.

"You can't expect me to take a trip like that and wear old clothes, Dad," Marcia wailed. "Everybody on the ship will just stare at me. I'll have to have my hair done, too. Right, Mother?"

"Of course you will, darling," Carol reassured her. "And so will I. There'll be loads of people on board. And I'll need a whole raft of things for Cindy and Bobby and Jan."

"Did I say this wasn't going to cost too much?" asked Mike in a dazed voice. "I must have been out of my mind."

The next two weeks seemed to fly by. Mike had to work extra hours at the office and past midnight at home in order to complete plans for a new warehouse. They were needed so the building crew could get to work before he got back from the cruise.

Carol had to spend most of her days shopping and there was a constant parade of visits to department stores in town. Nobody particularly wanted to go to the doctor to get the required injections against typhoid and typhus and smallpox. And for a time Cindy and Bobby absolutely refused to go because they hated the needles that would be stuck in their arms. But in the end they went because they knew they'd have to stay at home if they didn't.

Actually it wasn't too bad. Even Cindy was surprised at the fact that the doctor's needles didn't hurt much. They always looked as if they would. But when they went in under the skin you hardly felt them at all. Bobby said it was over before he really knew what was happening to him.

Meals were somewhat chancy because Alice was gone a good deal of the time too. So they made do with a lot of salads, like chicken salad and tunafish salad, and omelettes with cheese and without cheese and a few nights Mike just packed everybody into the car and took them to a nearby hamburger place because there just was not enough time to shop for food and to prepare it.

Then there was the necessary business of cutting the newspaper off so that prowlers would not notice the piled-up newspapers. The neighbors had to be asked to keep an eye on the house and to pick up the mail every day. And the telephone had to be "temporarily disconnected." Sometimes crooks called you and if you were not home all day, several days running, they figured they could break in safely and rob your house because you were probably out of town.

At night, long before normal bedtimes everybody was exhausted from all the chores and racing around, but nobody really minded. The kids pored over maps of the route their ship would take and talked about all the places they would stop at.

First the *Star of California* would stop at San Diego to pick up more people. Then it would move to Ensenada and La Paz in Lower California. Then it would cross the Gulf of California to Acapulco. Then it would cruise along the Pacific coast of Central America until they got to the Panama Canal.

They would go through the canal—and how that excited them all. "Imagine going through the Panama Canal. Wowie!" Bobby yelled as they studied the blue maps. And after that they would sail into the Caribbean and the West Indies, where the pirates had based their ships centuries ago.

Finally, to everyone's surprise—they still could not believe they were actually going till the last moment—they were ready to sail. The ship was due to leave at eleven and at six o'clock that morning they were all up, tearing around the house like wild animals, hunting madly for shoes, socks, books, cameras, pocket radios—all the paraphernalia people clutch at the last minute.

They drove down to the pier half asleep and hardly able to talk because each person was enjoying his or her fantasy about the trip. Greg was thinking about the marvelous-looking girls he would meet. The ship was bound to be loaded with gorgeous smooth-talking teen-aged girls and with luck he'd find a deck chair next to them. Marcia was thinking of all the dramatic clothes changes she would make. A new outfit at break-

14

fast, then one at lunch, and a third at dinner. And maybe there'd be a lovely dance to go to. Cruises usually had gala dances and carnival nights. She had heard all about them from a schoolmate who had gone on a cruise the year before.

The girl had described it as "absolutely super, Marcia, something new pops at you every night . . . nearly every hour almost."

As for Jan, she was thinking of all the deck sports she would enjoy, games she had read about like shuffleboard, but had never played. And it would be great taking long walks around the decks and swimming in the outdoor pools. And Peter was also thinking of the swimming and maybe going in the engine room and talking to the chief engineer, watching him oil the machines and operate them. Maybe the engineer would even let him push a few buttons or pull a few levers.

Cindy and Bobby were thinking about all the crazy stairways and rooms the new ship would have. Maybe even more than the *Queen Mary*. They could imagine what fun it would be to play hide-and-seek on the ship and to explore the different decks and public rooms, and of course the huge lifeboats. Cindy promised herself she would try the lifeboats the first chance she got.

As for Mike, he thought of the skeet shooting, where they catapulted clay pigeons out over the ocean and you tried to shoot them down. And he thought of the food. That would be fantastic. It always was on these cruises. He'd probably have to watch his weight or he'd come back looking like a small mountain.

Carol was looking forward to resting in a comfortable deck chair with a good book and looking up at regular intervals to enjoy the blue sea. And to breathe the smog-free air.

Alice pictured herself as just taking it easy. No cooking or cleaning to do and plenty of food to eat. And who could tell? This might be where she would meet the man she wanted to marry. Heaven knew that Sam the butcher back home couldn't make up his mind about her. Maybe "Mr. Right" would be in the next cabin or sitting in the next deck chair.

By the time they arrived all of them felt a pleasant glow of anticipation. The great sea adventure was actually getting underway. There was a constant flow of traffic around them as they checked their baggage and had their papers examined. And everyone else looked just as happy and as excited as they did. Or almost everybody.

As they waited at the foot of the gangplank, the Bradys suddenly noticed a commotion behind them. They turned to see two men arguing angrily with a cabdriver. One of them was tall and had red curly hair and wore sunglasses. In his very fashionable sports jacket and doeskin slacks and boots he looked like a bored movie star going on a vacation. The man with him was shorter and stockier, with wide eyes that had bags under them, and a heavy, dark growth of beard.

"Blow, Mac," the taller man said in a grim voice, "or I'll bend your skull like a pretzel. You're trying to steal us blind. I saw you take those detours to get here."

"That ain't true," the cabbie protested. "I took the shortest route."

"Take off, buddy, while you can walk," the shorter man said in a hoarse, threatening tone. He took a bill out of his pocket, crumpled it into a little ball, and threw it in the cabdriver's face. Then he pivoted on his heel and bumped into Greg as he struggled with two of the family bags.

"Why don't you open your eyes, kid," the short man said. "Next time you're liable to end up with a couple of cracked ribs."

He moved briskly toward the gangplank and nearly collided with Bobby, who was throwing a ball to Cindy as their parents waited on line to have their tickets checked by the purser.

"Watch it, kiddo," the man barked angrily. "I just had the suit cleaned. I don't want no dirty ball all over it!"

Jan frowned as she saw Bobby and Cindy move away frightened. She went over and patted her young brother and sister reassuringly.

"Don't listen to him, Bobby and Cindy. There's no law against playing here."

But privately she was worried about the two visitors. They didn't seem to fit in with all the happy people going on the ship. She felt a chill move down her spine as the short man's reptilian eyes bore in on her. Greg noticed her reaction.

17

"Boy I'd sure hate to meet that snake-eyed character in a dark alley," he told Jan. "I hope he isn't anywhere near our cabins."

"All aboard that's going aboard!" a hearty sailor's voice boomed suddenly.

Chapter *TWO*

Those magic words made them forget everything else. They were actually leaving the dock in half an hour! The Bradys finished filling out papers and scurried up the long gangplank and then down to their staterooms.

They had four rooms on "A" deck. In one were Mike and Carol Brady. In the next was Alice by herself. The three girls shared a third cabin and the fourth contained the three boys. The rooms were adjoining so that the family would be together. Yet because of their individual rooms, each felt alone and somewhat isolated.

Each cabin had three bunks except for Alice's which was a narrow single. In Mike's cabin there was a nice double bed and it made them feel as if they were at home. Or they did until they looked out at the blue ocean through the big glass-covered porthole. They relaxed, delighted to be on a ship.

The situation in the other staterooms was not quite as relaxed, however. Alice felt as if she were in a room that was only slightly bigger than a phone booth. She was able to adjust to that after a while. But she felt lonely in the room all by herself until she turned on her pocket radio and heard her favorite disc jockey.

In the Brady girls' stateroom, Marcia, Jan, and Cindy were having a tough time deciding who slept where. There were three bunks. Two were lower bunks and were really beds welded to the wall just a few feet above the ground. But the third was an upper and had to be reached by a ladder from the ground.

"Who takes what?" Marcia asked. "Does anybody have any preference before we decide?"

Cindy immediately opted for the top bunk. "I think it'll be wonderful just swaying back and forth while we're on the ocean, she explained. "And besides I don't mind the ladder."

But Jan wanted the top bed too, so Marcia broke up the argument by telling them they would draw lots. She wrote three names on tiny pieces of note paper and put them in a drawer of the bureau that came with the cabin. "You pick them out, Cindy, without looking. Whatever name comes up first gets first crack at the beds. Then the second name gets to pick and so on."

The others agreed and Cindy, closing her eyes, put her hand into the open drawer with

19

the folded notes. She drew her own name first and squealed with delight. Before anyone could try to change her mind, she scurried up the ladder and stretched out on her bed.

"Oh boy this is great," she told her sisters. "It's like sleeping on the roof."

Just at that moment the ship heaved and got underway. And since she was close to the edge of the bunk she nearly fell off.

"Want to move down to the lower one, Cindy?" Marcia asked her gently. "If there's a lot of rolling and pitching, you'll feel much safer. It's a short drop to the floor anyway."

Cindy blushed and nodded quickly. Marcia helped her little sister to get down and made her comfortable. Jan watched them closely, her face flushed with barely controlled excitement.

"Do you suppose we'll have any trouble with icebergs," she asked. "All we need is one of those and it's 'man the lifeboats.' We'll all have to jump off the boat in twenty minutes. Maybe even less. I saw a movie on TV once about a ship that——"

"Oh come on Jan," Marcia said, frowning. "Stop trying to scare the daylights out of us. Icebergs don't come this far south and if they did, they'd be too tiny to cause any trouble."

"Yes but we might still hit a whale," Cindy said. "I saw a cartoon once on TV where a ship hit a whale and nearly broke into two parts."

"Okay, okay," Marcia said, laughing. "And somebody might pull the plug out of the ocean in China on the other side of the world and let all the water out and then we'd sink to the bottom and have to put wheels on the hull to drive to Hong Kong. Or maybe the ship might melt in the hot sun the further south we go. Holy smoke, you could go on like this for hours. Stop worrying about the ship. It's a beautiful ship and it's almost new. It was built only four years ago."

Her younger sisters smiled sheepishly and said nothing for a moment. Then Cindy asked gently. "Hey I wonder what Greg, Peter, and Bobby are doing right this minute in their cabin?"

"Probably fighting like mad for who gets the top bunk." Jan offered. "And I'll bet Peter wins because he's the fastest."

She was wrong. Greg had taken the top bunk. Bobby had taken the lowest and Peter was right in the middle. And they weren't fighting. They were listening with great interest to the sounds coming from the bulkhead that separated their cabin from the next one.

At first they had indeed begun to squabble about the beds as the girls did. But in the midst of their arguing, they heard a man in the next room say, "SHUT UP, HARRY! THERE AIN'T NOTHING I CAN DO ABOUT IT!"

Greg, who had been unpacking his things, stopped with a shirt in his hand. He looked at Peter who was pulling out the drawers from a nearby bureau and Bobby, who was bouncing up and down on the lower bunk.

"I can't help it if those dumb kids are next door," the voice continued bitterly. "I tried to slip the purser a twenty-dollar bill to move them.

21

But he gave me some stupid jazz about they're being a family traveling together. He couldn't separate them no way. So what the hell could I do? I couldn't bop him over the head and make him. We'll just have to live with the stupid brats, that's all."

"Ssh!" Greg whispered to his brothers. "That's one of the tough-looking guys we ran into at the dock, remember? I recognize his voice."

The three Brady boys glued their ears to the wall.

"Well, I don't like it," another voice said. "It's going to make it tougher to work with Mary."

"Don't worry about it," a woman's voice chimed in. "I can always come in here on the sly when everybody's at dinner. We'll just skip the food or come in late."

"Those are the guys from the dock okay," Peter said excitedly. Greg waved furiously to him to keep quiet.

"Or we can meet in the upstairs bar, sort of casual like," Harry said. "Right, Lakey?"

The man addressed as Lakey was silent for a minute. Then he spoke decisively. Greg remembered him as the taller one.

"Yeah, yeah. I got an idea," he said suddenly. "See, we all meet in the bar later like we're just passing through. We don't know Mary when the thing comes off. Yeah that's good. Otherwise as soon as the jewels are gone, they'll be checking everybody in the room. We may all be searched."

Peter, Bobby, and Greg all stared at one another.

"Okay let's go over it again," Mary said impatiently. "I've got to get back before this dumb bunny I'm rooming with starts searching for me. I don't want to make her too suspicious. I told her I was traveling alone."

"All right," Lakey said. "First thing is for you to get close to the women. The ones I pointed out to you. All of them have registered their jewels for over a hundred thousand dollars each. I got the straight goods on that."

"You mean there are half a dozen women on this boat carrying over a hundred grand in ice?" Harry asked.

"Don't use the word 'ice,' you moron," Lakey said. "You might forget and use it in public. They'd put you down as a hood. We got an image to worry about. Don't say 'ice,' say 'jewels.' "

"Sorry, Lakey. But six women carrying all that ice—er jewels. That's more than we bargained for."

"There may be even more, dummy!" Lakey said. "A lot of older women, rich women especially, take these cruises just to show off. They get themselves a lot of expensive clothes, buy top-notch jewelry, and live it up. They're loaded to the gills with diamond bracelets and pearl necklaces every night."

"Good," the woman called Mary said, laughing. "We'll help lighten their load by taking their jewelry away."

"Right," Lakey said, chuckling. "But first we

23

do our homework. Get close to the old biddies who registered the jewels with the purser's office. Here's the list, Mary. You can let us know when the best time is to pull the heist and then we're off to the races."

"Terrific," Harry said. "We won't have to pull another heist for at least a year. With all the loot we'll get in this one."

"Listen I'd better go," Mary said quickly. "I'm late now. Suppose we meet in the bar, like right before dinner. Say fiveish, okay? Then we'll pretend we're just meeting."

"Right, kid," Lakey said. "Keep cool, baby. This is going to be a lead pipe cinch. They'll never know what hit them."

"And meanwhile we can live it up ourselves," Harry added. "What the hell, we're paying for it right?"

"Okay," Lakey said. "But watch the boozing, Harry. I got no room for drunks on this caper. I've been waiting a long time for this thing to come off. See you later," Lakey added. "And good luck with your research. This heist may set a record for stealing jewelry on the high seas. Half a million dollars. Whew!"

Greg pulled Peter and Bobby to the center of the cabin and whispered to them. "Did you guys hear that? They're planning to pull the biggest jewel robbery on the high seas."

"What are we going to do?" Peter asked.

"Let's tell Dad and Mom," Bobby said.

"Good idea," Greg said. "But let's do it fast."

Chapter *THREE*

~~~~~~~~~~~~~~~~

Ten minutes later the boys repeated the over-heard conversation to their mother and father. The adults listened carefully and then exchanged smiles.

"What's the matter, Dad?" Greg asked. "Why are you smiling?"

"Because it's the most ridiculous story I ever heard. I think you must have imagined the whole thing." Mike laughed.

"But we heard it, Dad," Bobby insisted.

"Then you were being kidded," Carol said. "Now, why don't you just forget about it and take a walk around the ship with us, dear."

"No, Mom," Peter said. "I think we have to tell the captain about this. It might be serious."

"Peter, I think whoever said those things—if he said them—was just playing a joke on you. You're just going to make yourself look foolish repeating it to the captain," Carol said.

"Well, I want to tell him anyway. Is it okay?" Peter asked.

Carol and Make sighed and nodded. "Just don't take up too much of his time with it," Mike said. "He's got much more serious things to think about. But go ahead if you have to."

"Let's go, Peter and Bobby," Greg said. "The sooner we get to the captain's cabin the better. No telling how fast these guys are going to move."

Carol and Mike watched them race out of the room and laughed. "Maybe we ought to warn the captain," she said. Mike brushed the idea away with his hand. "He's heard wilder stories than this, I'm sure. Besides, it may amuse him."

Outside, the three boys stopped a passing steward and asked him the way to the captain's cabin. They moved quickly down the corridors. On the way they nearly collided with Lakey.

He stared at them angrily but said nothing.

"Wow," Peter said. "I hope he doesn't know where we're headed. We're only about fifty yards from the captain's room."

"Ssh," Greg warned. "He might hear you. Pipe down."

A moment later they were outside the captain's cabin. They looked around to see if Lakey were in sight but he had gone around the corner. Getting up his courage, Greg knocked on the door. It was opened by a young man in blues hardly older than Greg himself.

"Yes?" the boy said politely.

"Can we see the captain, please?" Greg asked.

"Well he's rather busy right now. Can it wait till later?"

"No," Bobby shot out. "They may rob them blind by that time."

The boy in the blue uniform looked puzzled. "Who will?"

"The guys next door," Peter chimed in. "We heard the whole thing. They're planning a record jewel robbery on the high seas."

The uniformed boy looked anxiously at the empty corridor and then hastened to let them enter.

"Better come in," he said.

"What's all that noise at the door?" a hearty voice boomed from the other side of the large room. "I'm trying to study some charts here."

"It's some boys, sir," the uniformed lad said. "They want to talk to you about a robbery being planned on board."

"Bring them over here," rasped the voice.

Peter, Greg, and Bobby moved across the large, many-windowed room and stood before a large table filled with maps. Hovering over the table was an enormous man, well over six feet. Dark whiskers covered much of his lower face but his blue eyes twinkled at them.

"Okay let's have it," he said tersely. "Who's planning a robbery aboard my ship?"

Greg, Peter, and Bobby began to speak all at once.

"One at a time," bellowed the captain. He pointed a long forefinger at Greg. "You be the spokesman. If there's anything more to add when you've finished, they can talk all they like."

Slowly Greg repeated the conversation. The captain asked him if he could be certain who said what.

"Well not really," Greg said uncomfortably. "They were all talking together, you see. But their voices sounded familiar."

"You know these men?" the captain asked.

"Well not really, Captain," Greg said, squirming under his gaze. "But we did hear them talk at the dock just before we boarded the ship. I never met the woman. We don't know who she is. We're not sure about her."

"Can either of you identify who spoke," the captain asked the younger boys. "This is a pretty serious charge you're making."

Peter and Bobby hesitated, then sheepishly shook their heads. They did not remember the voices on the docks as well as did Greg.

"We're not really too sure," Peter said disappointedly. "But I know we heard those men next door say they're planning a big robbery."

"I don't think you're too sure about anything," the captain snapped. "Sit down on that sofa while I make a telephone call." He frowned. "This better not be a joke!"

They sat down worriedly while the captain seized the telephone in his hamlike fist. They heard him ask the purser several questions about the men in the cabin next to theirs and then sit quietly with the instrument glued to his ear. The look on his face frightened them all. His chin was thrust forward menacingly as he listened and his eyes roamed over their faces as if he wanted to remember them for the future.

"Let's get out of here," Bobby whispered in a

scared voice. "I don't like the way he's looking us over. Let's just walk out."

"Yeah," Peter said. "We can just pretend it never happened. We're not really that sure it was the men on the dock anyway."

As he spoke he got off the couch and began to move toward the door. Bobby moved in unison with them. Greg motioned them to sit down. He started to speak but before a word could issue from his mouth, the strong voice of the ship's leader boomed over their heads.

"Get back on that sofa, you two," the captain yelled. "And see that you stay there!"

The boys sat down quickly. Bobby felt his heart beating wildly as the captain stood over them. Peter had to fight a mad impulse to cut and run from the room. Even Greg felt uneasy as the huge bewhiskered face loomed over them.

"The men in the cabin next to yours are legitimate businessmen. They own a chain of travel agencies in the United States and they do a lot of business with the firm that owns this vessel. I am sure you boys were mistaken and I am not going to embarrass them by inquiring further into this matter.

"I don't know what you think you overheard but the whole thing is utter nonsense. The purser knows a good deal about these men and they could make a great deal of trouble for you if you repeat this story to anyone."

"But, Captain, I tell you I heard them planning the whole thing," Greg protested.

"My advice to you, young man—what is your name by the way?"

"Greg . . . Greg Brady."

The captain's eyes flashed angrily at him. "I've got to get back to my charts now. My advice to you is to forget the entire thing. I think if you publicize this story any further, they might even make trouble for your parents. You say your parents advised you to tell this fantastic tale to me?"

"Not exactly," Grey said reluctantly.

"Good afternoon, boys," the captain said firmly. He turned his back to them. Then he began to shake with laughter. "This is the most absurd nonsense I've ever heard. You probably heard some radio sketch before we left shore. Incidentally," they heard him say as they reached the door of the cabin. "If this story makes the rounds of this ship and you have no further proof than you've given me now," he paused for effect, "well, according to the purser, these men might sue your parents in court for being a party to slander. For trying to damage their reputations."

As they turned to open the door, the captain spoke again, unable to control his laughter.

"Of course if you learn any more fairy tales like that and tell them—to me privately in confidence, that's quite another matter, boys." The captain's eyes twinkled with humor. "I'm always willing to be entertained by interesting stories. Goodbye, boys."

As soon as they closed the door behind them,

the three Brady boys moved as fast as they could for the open deck. When they were at the rail over the swirling blue waves, they breathed more easily.

"Whew, I'm sure glad that's over," Peter said. "I thought he'd throw us all in the brig or something."

"Yeah, nothing but bread and water till we reached land," Bobby said. "I'm really glad it's over."

"It's not over," Greg said firmly. "You heard what the captain said. If we hear anything else or learn anything new, he'd like to hear about it."

"Yeah, so he could be entertained," grinned Peter. "But I didn't like what he said about Mom and Dad being sued in court."

"Right," Greg said, his jaw set. "So we don't repeat this to anyone else. Except maybe the girls. Cause we might need their help. But somehow we're going to get to the bottom of this. I'm not going to let those guys get away with it." He frowned. "And I don't like being laughed at like I'm a nitwit either."

He looked at his brothers. "Listen, you don't have to help me if you don't want to. I mean if you're scared I'll understand all right. Just say so."

Peter and Bobby looked at one another. "I want to help you," Peter said quickly.

"Me too," said Bobby.

Greg smiled. "Okay. Here's what we do. We'll let the girls keep watch on the woman in the cabin next to ours. And we three will watch the two men."

"But we don't know what the woman looks like," Peter said.

"We'll find out very soon. Come on with me," Greg said.

They went to the girls' cabin and told their sisters about the planned jewel robbery. Greg was amused by their reactions. Marcia smiled in disbelief as she brushed back her long hair. Jan brought her palms together in delight. The whole story seemed to be too much for her. As for little Cindy, her eyes widened till they looked as big as saucers.

Greg then explained how he wanted them to help. Marcia slapped the bed with delight. "Wow!"

"That mean yes you will help or no?" Jan asked, looking puzzled.

"You kidding?" Marcia said. "Me miss a big adventure on the high seas?" She grinned up at her big brother. "Brother Greg, you just got yourself a new female private eye."

"Two of them," Jan said.

"Four," Cindy piped up. "You can have both of mine."

"Right," Greg said happily. "Okay here's what we do. We all move down to the bar where they meet in a few minutes. But we do it carefully so as not to be noticed. Each of us goes in separately and looks at the three of them. Got that? I want you all to study their faces so you don't lose them in a crowd. From now on we keep a tight stakeout on them. They don't go anywhere without one of us right with them. Okay?"

"Okay," everyone said at the same time.

"What happens if they catch us?" Cindy asked a little worriedly.

"Yeah, they can be pretty angry if they find out we've tailed them," Peter remarked.

"This is strictly a volunteer assignment," Greg said in the tone of a military commander. "You're in or you're out as you wish. But once you're in you follow orders just like good soldiers. These guys are planning a big robbery, but we have to prove it's coming off before the captain will do anything to them."

Everyone was in. A moment later they moved in pairs, fifteen yards apart to the bar. Each person walked inside alone as if he or she were looking for someone. Inside the semidarkened bar they saw Lakey and Harry and an attractive blond girl in her twenties. As they each entered, the three conspirators turned their heads to look at them with interest, then just as quickly turned back again. If they thought it odd that six youngsters should come in one by one, they said nothing.

But the bartender was another matter. After the third kid, Jan, had entered, he asked her politely but curiously what she wanted in the bar. Jan was so flustered by his question that she asked him shyly for a glass of water. The three conspirators, who were talking in the opposite corner, eyed her warily.

The next two days and nights one of the

Bradys was near them night and day. Whether the three conspirators were at the bar or sitting on deck chairs or walking the decks or even in the swimming pool, they had little eyes watching them. Someone was always behind them, taking care not to get too close.

Greg tried to be fair, of course. Each of the kids was given an hour or two of following them and the rest of the time he or she was off and could enjoy the ship. And there was much to enjoy. The deck was full of activity all day. People constantly moving to and fro, playing shuffleboard or other games. Or it was fun to watch Mike Brady and other men shoot at the clay pigeons that were catapulted over the blue sea by a machine on deck.

On hot days—and they were getting hotter as the ship moved further south—crowds thronged the two swimming pools on the vessel. The kids played rousing games of water polo in the water or just raced each other from one side to the other.

And there was loads to eat at all times. The Brady kids had never seen such mountains of fantastic food in all their lives. The list of desserts alone was enormous. It included pies, cakes, baked Alaska, cherries jubilee, plum pudding, nearly twenty flavors of ice cream, sundaes of many varieties, and several European desserts they had never even heard of.

And the rest of the menu was almost stupefying. At breakfast for example they could have ham, bacon, eggs, pancakes, waffles, kippered herring, fresh rolls, doughnuts, jelly rolls, coffee-cake, pies, and enough varieties of hot and cold cereals to fill a supermarket shelf across the width of the store. The ship seemed, indeed, to have been designed as a heaven for eaters. Anything that the human mind or stomach could desire was there in great quantity.

There was nothing to do but enjoy yourself on the boat, it seemed, and it was this that made it hard for the Brady Bunch to do a careful job of watching the jewel thieves. From morning to night they were pampered and treated like lazy kings on holiday and it caught them off balance.

First, there was the enormous breakfast just described. Peter and Jan, especially, ate so much cake and tried so many cereals that they felt sleepy the rest of the morning. Quite often, even after Greg begged them to watch the two men or the woman, they would fall asleep on a deck chair. Once Greg and Marcia came by to relieve them and found them snoring away in the brisk ocean breeze, completely oblivious to whatever was going on around them.

And it was not just Peter and Jan. All of them felt like fat old sheep dogs who did nothing. True there were two swimming pools on board, a fine gymnasium, and all sorts of nice games for the passenger. But who could find the energy for all these things after all that food? Lunch was the same mountain of foods as breakfast and at three there were snacks offered by the busy stewards—delicious little sandwiches and cakes with milk or coffee. Then a few hours later there was dinner, which was again a gigantic meal. This meal dwarfed all the others.

The feast here started with various appetizers, like shrimp cocktail, lobster on the shell, herrings in cream with slices of apple, and then moved on to a wide list of soups: lentil soup, chicken soup, vichyssoise, shrimp soup, bouillabaisse or fish soup, numerous types of spaghetti, like fettuccine, spaghetti with anchovies, with eggs and bacon, lasagna, cannelloni, and much more. Then there were roasts, steaks, rare meat like venison, or deer meat laced with wild strawberries, goose cooked with green grapes and sweet purple cabbage, and lots more the Bradys had never heard of.

They were astonished by the amount of everything. Even Alice, who had begun by vowing to keep on a strict diet and Carol Brady, who had made the same promise, were amazed.

"We won't be able to get into the new dresses we're going to buy when we get back home. So we're sticking to just a few snacks like plain old steaks and broiled fish and absolutely no desserts," Carol explained to her husband.

And then, when they caught sight of things like moist brioches and other cakes garlanded with glazed fruit blossoms, cakes filled with poached pears in a sea of vanilla sauce, they felt sorry they had made their vows to diet. When they were confronted at neighboring tables with masterpieces made by the pastry chef on board, fantastic things to eat like sugar matadors, and windmills, birds made of pure candy, baked

Alaskas, lemon soufflé surrounded by pear ice cream with a raspberry purée, and tiny boats made of almonds and filled with delicious peach ice cream, they went out of their minds.

Pretty soon the older Bradys and Alice were competing with the kids to see who could order the most bizarre foods—because anything you asked for simply came from the vast kitchen. After the first day they were asking excitedly for Polish ham, Danish bacon, quiche Lorraines, and the sort of desserts that made their mouths water just to think of.

After all that glorious eating—and there was another late snack buffet at nine—they went around all day feeling very logy and with their eyes half closed. When they weren't eating, they were seeing the latest movies (some of them still not released in the theaters), or listening to good music or dancing.

A social director on the ship had planned daily sessions of classical and rock music, dances, and evening games. The adults were also invited to various cocktail parties given by the captain or other people on the ship. It seemed that all you had to do to throw a party was tell your steward and he brought you loads of food, canapés on platter, little frankfurters, platters of shrimp, pastrami, corned beef and tongue, little buckets of cheese, cookies, cakes, liquor, soda pop, and anything else you needed to entertain with. All you were charged for was the hard liquor and other spirits.

For a few days, the Brady kids were so busy

rushing about the ship, eating, visiting parties, and playing games that they almost forgot about the jewel thieves. Then one day Marcia overheard Mary, the girl who was in cahoots with the thieves, reveal exactly how they were going to move after the jewels.

It was the afternoon of the fourth day out. The *Star of California* was moving through the warm seas off the Pacific coast of Mexico. As usual, the Brady kids had done little but enjoy an easygoing life that day. After breakfast they had gone for long walks around the deck. The three boys competed with their sisters to see who would make it back to a certain point on the top deck. They all started from the same point but the girls went around the ship in one direction and the boys in another. The girls won easily.

There had been some swimming in the outdoor pool and then a long lazy lunch. Then a nap on a deck chair with the sea breeze moving placidly over their faces. About four o'clock, Mike Brady came to where they were sitting and said they had all been invited to a party half an hour later.

"Who?" the kids all asked excitedly.

"A Mr. and Mrs. Arthur J. Bailey. They're traveling with their children, Harry and Doris, who go to the same school as Greg and Marcia," Carol Brady told them.

"Oh, are they here too?" Greg asked excitedly. Marcia's eyes lit up with great pleasure.

"Well that's wonderful," Marcia said. "I know Harry. He's a terrific guy, a fantastic personality, and a wonderful dancer."

"That's fine," Mike said, smiling at Carol and Alice. "Because you'll have a chance to see him. He'll be there and so will Doris."

"Hey that's super," Greg blurted out, unable to conceal his joy. "I've been wanting to date that girl all year. Trouble is she's so popular, you can't get near her on campus." He blushed deeply as he saw Peter and Jan giggle at his obvious excitement.

Well, I'm delighted you like them," Carol said. "It should make the trip nicer for both of you."

"How did they know we were on the same ship?" Peter asked, puzzled. "I mean there are so many people."

"Oh that's simple," Mike said. "Anybody can consult a passenger list in the purser's office. People do that because they want to hold these parties. Well, Mr. Bailey called us right after lunch and said that he's having a party for many people. And he wanted all of us because you two go to school with their kids.

"Yeah, we'd better be nice to Greg and Marcia," Alice said laughing, "or they won't let us in. We're just being invited to the big clambake because their kids are nuts about our two lovebirds."

"Aw, come on, Alice," Greg said, deeply embarrassed. "Don't start pulling that stuff at the party or I won't stay. I have to run into Doris in school all year round. We're even in a couple of activities together. I couldn't even speak to her if you started stuff like that."

"Neither could I," Marcia said uneasily. "Beside it would make Harry feel terribly swellheaded if he thought I'd complimented him. It'd be impossible to do anything with him. And we're in the drama club together too."

"Oh stop fretting," Alice said. "I won't tell either of them you nearly fell overboard when you heard they were on the ship."

After that conversation, the kids nearly fell over themselves racing back to their cabins to get dressed. They sailed into the Bailey suite of rooms about forty minutes later. Greg had put on his best sports jacket and slacks and even wore a shirt and new tie, something he normally hated to do. As for Marcia, she wore her prettiest dress, a magnificent concoction of blue with red trimmings and several pieces of costume jewelry her mother had loaned her.

The other kids and the adults were well dressed but not as scrumptiously. They weren't trying to impress anyone. But if Marcia and Greg marched in with delight, their pleasure changed to sheer astonishment as soon as they entered.

For there smack in the center of the room were the three jewel thieves: Lakey, Harry, and Mary.

Chapter *FOUR*

≈≈≈≈≈≈≈≈≈≈≈≈≈≈≈≈≈≈≈

The three conspirators were standing in the midst of more than fifty people who were laughing, drinking, and buzzing with the loud, excited chatter that usually is heard at such afternoon parties.

"Hi Greg," a young, vibrant, and familiar voice yelled as soon as the Bradys entered. Greg smiled foolishly as a very pretty dark-haired girl in a swirling white tennis outfit danced up to them.

"I just flipped when I heard you were on the ship," she said, taking both his hands. "I mean isn't it fantastic, being together on the same cruise and all. When I saw your name I thought it was an error. I just couldn't believe it."

She waved to a tall man with graying temples and to a stout woman beside him. "Hey Mom, Dad. Come over and meet the guy I told you about."

Greg flushed a deep red as the other people in the room turned to look at him with curiosity. He saw Lakey and Harry's eyes widen with surprise as they recognized him.

Marcia gripped Greg's arm to steady him. She

41

was just as shocked as he to see Lakey, Harry, and Mary. They exchanged quick looks with Peter, Jan, Bobby, and Cindy. Watching all this, Mike Brady frowned, but they said nothing to him. And indeed they had no time even if they had wanted to.

The Baileys soon descended on them in a flurry of greetings and welcomes and handshakes. Out of the corner of his eye, Greg could see the surprise registered on the faces of the two men they had quarreled with at the dock. Marcia had no time to even look. Young Harry Bailey was so delighted to see her that he pulled her over to one side of the room to talk to her.

"Hey, what are you all doing on this boat?" he asked, his blue eyes shining. "I didn't expect to see you till the fall. What part of the ship you staying on?"

The questions poured out of him as he looked at her. Meanwhile Greg was talking busily to Harry's sister. Peter, disgusted with both of his family lovebirds, decided to take matters into his own hands. Somebody had to keep tabs on the crooks. It was a cinch it couldn't be Greg or Marcia and he didn't trust the other kids to give the matter the concentration the job deserved, so he decided to do it himself.

He began by circling idly around the big stateroom, reaching out for cookies and nuts on the table, drinking a tall glass of punch and pretending to be interested in the gay atmosphere of the party. After about ten minutes of this, he approached Mary, who was talking to a big fat man in a white suit. Peter, being careful not to let his interest be obvious to them, looked the other way as he munched on an almond and chocolate cookie.

The fat man's sheeplike eyes brushed his own for a second, then moved back to the girl.

"You're all set on the time and place then, Mary?" he whispered.

Mary looked at the fat man anxiously. "Why don't we walk outside for a minute? I think I need some fresh air."

"Of course my dear," the fat man in the white suit said soothingly. "It's a bit stuffy in here with the cigarette smoke and all these people. Let's by all means take a little stroll around the deck."

A moment later the couple left. As they shut the cabin door behind them, Peter looked anxiously at Greg and tried desperately to get him to come over. But it was impossible. Old Greg was so happy with his silly girlfriend, Peter thought bitterly, that he didn't care that one of the conspirators was getting away. Not only that. She was probably on the point of spilling everything about the robbery.

"Greg!" Peter said, coming closer to him. "Can I talk to you for a minute."

"I'm busy," Greg said, smiling at Doris as they stood very close to one another. "Can't it wait till later?"

"No, it can't wait till later," Peter said crossly. "Ever hear the one about locking the barn after your horse is stolen?"

"What the heck are you talking about?" Greg asked, his eyes frowning. "Is this one of your corny jokes again, Peter?" He laughed appreciatively at Doris, who was grinning at them both. "You have to excuse my brother here. He sometimes falls into strange languages that none of us understands."

"Well, try to understand this!" answered Peter. "The bird has just flown the coop with her partner and they're headed for a little nest outside where she's going to sing him the whole song."

"Wha—a–at?" Greg asked, completely puzzled. "What's all this about birds and coops and singing? Have you gone and flipped your lid, little brother, or what?"

"Oh skip it!" Peter said, completely frustrated. "Maybe Marcia can understand what I'm trying to tell you."

He turned on his heel and broke through the crowd of people milling about them. Where on earth was his sister, Marcia, he asked himself disgustedly.

For what seemed like ages, he could find no sign of her anywhere. Had she left the cabin as well, he wondered. Just when he was about to give up in disgust, he saw her and Harry Bailey standing in a corner. Harry was a tall, almost incredibly thin boy with a large head. He had not seen his sister's face because it was hidden behind Harry Bailey's head.

At first he could not even get her attention. She was giggling at everything dumb Harry was

44

telling her. What in heck does she see in that guy, Peter wondered. He wasn't especially good-looking or anything.

"Hey Marcia!" Peter said urgently. "Come over here; I want to talk to you."

He was answered by a smile of greeting from her, but it soon became clear that she had not heard a thing because of the din that was coming from the crowded room.

He waved to her in a frantic way, but when she saw the gesture, she looked at him helplessly, as if to say, "What can I do? Harry Bailey's got me trapped."

Peter looked daggers at her and if looks could have hurt anyone, at that instant his eyes could have pushed Harry Bailey right through the cabin porthole. Just as he was turning away, however, and giving up, he saw Greg windmilling to him from the other side of the room. There was no doubt about it now. Greg was waving madly to him.

He moved back toward his older brother and met him halfway.

"Hey, Peter I just got your meaning," Greg said a little breathlessly. "I just didn't connect the song of the birds with our little crooks, that's all. Where did they go?"

"I don't know. That's what I came over to tell you. They slipped out very suddenly right after he asked her if they had set the time and the place."

Greg's eyes widened with surprise, "Hey, we got to get to them fast. Very fast."

"Well, let's go," Peter said, annoyed. "They'll be on the other side of the ship while we stand here and talk about it."

Greg looked embarrassed.

"I'm sorry, Peter. I guess I just got a little too involved with Doris. Give me a few minutes to get squared away with her. Okay?"

Peter looked at him in amazement. "Can't you get squared away with Doris tomorrow, Greg? I mean, she isn't leaving the ship or anything, is she?"

Greg blushed deeply and stared at Doris, who was smiling and beckoning to him from the other end of the room. She was the prettiest girl in the room, he thought. Especially in that wonderful red dress she was wearing. It made her look like a movie star.

"Peter," Greg said firmly. "It won't take too long, I promise you. I'll be back in a few minutes and then we'll take care of everything." He grinned at Peter's gloomy face. "Aw, come on, Peter, don't look like that. I'll be right back."

Peter turned to look at Marcia's equally embarrassed face.

"I just heard what you said to Greg," she said. "And I'm sorry I was busy with Harry when you waved to me. I tried to come right over, but Harry kept talking and talking. You know how it is, Peter. Just give me a couple of minutes to work things out with Harry."

"Oh boy, you lovebirds sure make me sick," Peter said disgustedly.

"I think Harry is going to ask me to the junior

prom," said Marcia. "But he sure isn't going to do it if I just get up and walk out on him. The whole reason we came to this party was because he and Doris begged their folks to invite us all. Please, Peter."

"I thought you guys wanted to keep a tight stakeout on these people?" Peter asked.

"We do," Marcia said, "and we'll get after them just as soon as Greg and I get back. You wait right here, we'll only be a minute."

As soon as Greg and Marcia walked across the room, Peter waved to Jan, Bobby, and Cindy to meet with him outside. He wasn't going to wait for either Greg or Marcia.

Outside the cabin, Peter, grim-faced and determined, spoke like the coach of a professional football team in the last quarter of the game.

"All right, this is it. We gotta find them and fast. If we learn what they're up to, when they plan to steal the jewels, we might be able to stop them. Here's what we do. Cindy and I will walk along this deck and see if they're around. Jan, you and Bobby move along the deck above this one. If you come to the end and can't find them, go down to the deck just below this one.

"You can't miss them. The man is big and fat and he's wearing a white suit. He's almost bald too. The girl is tall and blond. That's what you got to look for. Now scoot."

As the Brady kids moved along the deck, the ship rolled and they had to steady themselves at the rails.

For twenty minutes each team scoured the

decks very thoroughly. They looked in all the ship's lounges, checked the people sitting in deck chairs with blankets around them, and even looked at the hatches or staircases. The result was zero. They had just about decided that Mary and her fat friend had probably gone into some cabin when Jan suddenly had an idea. She turned excitedly to Bobby.

"You know what we have to do, Bobby? We have to ask ourselves where would be the best place to hide if we wanted nobody to find us on deck."

"That's right. Some place where people don't walk much or sit down," Bobby said. "But where? We've looked all over. I don't think there is such a place."

"Yes there is," Jan persisted. Over there," she pointed. "See where they have those big big funnels. That's for the smoke to come out. If they stood just between the two funnels, nobody could really spot them. Unless they were right on top of them. And there's no reason to go there. The games and the lounge rooms are all on this side."

"I think you're right," Bobby said, eyeing his sister with admiration. "But how do we get over there without being seen ourselves? I mean, won't they be suspicious if they see strangers turn up there? Even if they don't go away, they sure won't keep talking if they think we can hear them."

Jan's forehead wrinkled while she gave the

matter some serious thought. Suddenly her face was all smiles.

"I've got it," she said triumphantly. "If we hide ourselves in one of the lifeboats right near them, we can hear them fine. And we'll be under the canvas top, so they won't be able to see us."

Her face fell. "There's just one thing. How do we get into the boat without their seeing us?"

Bobby thought about this too. "Hey, why don't we get some help from Peter and Cindy. They're coming up that staircase now. Maybe they can make some noise or something and we can duck in the boat while they're trying to find out who did it."

"Great idea," Jan said. She ran over to Peter and Cindy to tell them of the new plan to create a diversion.

Peter was delighted with it. "Hey, we don't need those lovebirds at all," he crowed. "We can do the whole thing ourselves. Okay let's do it. If they're there, I'll give you a signal. I'll raise my handkerchief and you move quickly toward the lifeboat. Meanwhile Cindy and I will kick up the biggest fuss you ever heard. They'll see us but they won't see you because they'll be looking in the opposite direction."

Jan crossed her fingers and said, "I hope that's where they are right now."

Holding their breaths, Jan and Bobby waited while they looked at the funnel area. Suddenly they saw Peter waving his white handkerchief frantically. The two Brady kids shot toward the huge funnels like bullets.

49

When they reached the rail alongside the twin funnels, they heard Cindy shouting angrily at Peter to give her back her watch.

"It's my watch," she screamed. "Give it back to me."

"No, he gave it to me," Peter yelled back just as loudly. "It's mine!"

"IT'S MINE, IT'S MINE," shouted Cindy.

As they continued to fight over the watch, Bobby ran, crouching low and shooting straight for the covered lifeboat just a couple of feet from the funnels. He climbed in quickly and waved to Jan to follow him. In another moment, she had raced to the same boat and climbed in.

As soon as they were inside, they could hear the voices of the two crooks clearly. They were speaking about the jewel robbery and how they were going to do it.

Chapter FIVE

≈≈≈≈≈≈≈≈≈≈≈≈≈

"Never mind those dumb brats," the man was saying. "We have to decide once and for all when we pull the job. There isn't time to fool around. Besides I got to send Ralph a message to let him know if we can give him the jewels in Puerto Rico."

"You hear that?" Bobby whispered, almost beside himself with excitement. "They're going to give someone the jewels in Puerto Rico. The ship goes there, right?"

"Ssh!" Jan said quickly. "They might hear you if you speak too loud. Yes, we stop there. Let's listen some more."

"Look, Oscar," the woman said impatiently. "Do we have to stand here yapping. There's a terrible draft here. And you know how easily I catch cold. All I need's the flu or something now —that'll ruin everything."

"I'm sorry, Mary," Oscar said testily. "I didn't want to go to my cabin or yours because they might be bugged."

"What makes you think the cabins would be bugged?" Mary demanded.

"Simple. Our contact on the staff found out about it. Seems those ratty kids, the Brady kids, went in and complained about Lakey and Harry to the captain. They have the cabin next to theirs, you know."

"If I ever get my hands on those kids," Mary said angrily, "I'll . . . I'll . . ."

"You won't do anything," Oscar broke in, annoyed. "Look, you dum-dum. How many times do I have to tell you. We're trying to pull a caper of half a million dollars. You think I'm going to endanger our whole plan by letting you go after some dumb kids."

"All I meant was——" Mary began.

"Leave them alone," Oscar said irritably. "Nobody believed them anyway. The captain threw

51

out the whole story when he heard it and the kids may have already forgot the whole deal. Probably think they imagined the conversation from Harry and Lakey. They're too busy having fun to worry about some jewels belonging to people they don't even know anyway."

"Okay, so how do we proceed, Oscar?" Mary asked.

"Simple. Two ways. Shortly after we cross through the Panama Canal, the captain usually throws a big party for all the first-class passengers. The women wear all their most expensive jewels. It's expected of them. We wait till the party's really swinging. Everybody's had something to drink and the music and activity all distract them. Then we move. We pull the jewels from the women and hide them somewhere in the room till the commotion dies down. After that we get the stuff off the boat. In Puerto Rico."

The excitement in the lifeboat had reached its peak. Bobby could not stay still any longer. He wanted to run to tell Peter and Greg and Marcia and Cindy. They had heard it all. The whole plan. They knew exactly how the big jewel robbery would happen and when.

"Where are you going, Bobby?" Jan asked, annoyed.

"To find the others. We have to tell them."

"We're not through here yet," Jan told him. "They're still talking."

"I'm sorry, Jan," Bobby said, apologizing. "I thought that was it."

"Ssh, they're still saying something and I want to hear it."

Oscar was telling Mary that the women to watch must be carefully cultivated.

"Get to know them all. Be very friendly with them, Mary," the fat man advised. "Get on a first-name basis. This way on the night of the caper we can all meet them, maybe dance with them, or sit down at their tables. It makes it much easier to get closer to them at the right time."

"We're still using the same list or are there any others added?"

"No," Oscar said. "The same list. If there are any changes, I'll let you know."

"You're still going to get the jewels the same way we planned?" Mary asked, laughing. "Isn't that a bit risky? With all those people around?"

Oscar laughed hoarsely. "Just remember, darling, they are not going to expect it."

He sighed. "Well I guess that's it. Any questions?"

"No, I don't think so," she said.

"Okay. Here's the complete list of the women's cabins and their phone extensions there. Also the names of friends in their home towns whom you could say told you that they might be on board. You're on your own."

"How about our contacts with the ship's crew?" Mary asked.

"They'll be meeting you. But be careful not to be seen talking about these matters with any of them. We may still be followed, you know. But

53

I know the captain didn't believe those silly kids."

"To think that they could ruin the whole deal for us!" Mary said angrily.

"Don't be silly, darling," Oscar said soothingly. "Those kids are too dumb to do anything of the kind. Just remember, sweetie, they're not dealing with amateurs. And if we aren't good enough to deal with some stupid young punks, then we'd better get out of the business altogether."

"Did you hear that?" Bobby said angrily. "You hear what he called us?"

"Yes," Jan said. "And they'll be very sorry when we turn them over to cops later."

"I'm going to tell Greg," Bobby said excitedly. "Boy, wait till he hears all this."

"Not yet, Bobby," she pleaded. "Let them leave first. They might see us."

But Bobby was too excited to listen to her. He turned irritably to her. "You heard them. They're all finished."

She pulled at his leg gently. "Not yet, Bobby."

"Why? Because you want to be the first to tell him?" he asked grinning at her in the darkness under the tarpaulin cover.

"Don't be silly," she said, exasperated with him. "You stay here till I tell you to leave!"

But Bobby did not like his sister's tone and quickly slid one foot over the edge of the lifeboat.

"Bobby, they'll see you!" she whispered loudly.

But Bobby was already out of earshot and

heard nothing. He was thinking only of how astonished Greg and Peter and Marcia and Cindy would be when he told them everything.

He not only did not hear Jan. He did not hear Mary when she spoke to Oscar.

"Oscar! Isn't that the kid we saw at the party?"

Oscar turned to look. "Yes I think he is. What's he doing here?"

"That's what I want to know. Do you suppose he was following us?"

Oscar was silent for a moment. "I'm not sure. He may just have been passing through. But I still don't like it."

"What are we going to do?" Mary asked anxiously.

"We can't take chances. Tell the others that we'll put the other plan into effect instead. Plan B. They may have overheard what we said here. But in any case, they don't know anything about plan B. We didn't even mention it once."

"You think it will work?" Mary asked.

"I don't know. But it's worth trying. With luck we'll be able to get quite a few jewels that way."

Chapter SIX

〰〰〰〰〰〰〰

Immediately after she heard Oscar's words, Jan knew there had to be a meeting of the Brady Bunch. It was absolutely necessary. As soon as the coast was clear, she made her way back to the party in the Baily stateroom. It was still going strong. In fact it seemed more crowded than ever.

To her disgust, she saw Bobby digging his face into a huge piece of cream cake at the big table laden with food. What a nitwit, she thought. Here they were confronted with a new problem, a new robbery plan they knew nothing about, and what was Bobby doing? He was stuffing his face with whipped cream and cake.

She scoured the full room for a sign of Marcia or Greg. As she looked, she heard her name called and turned to face her mother and father.

"Hey, Jan," Mike Brady said. "Where've you been?"

"Everyone's been asking for you," Carol told her. "We had no idea where you'd gone. Or Bobby for that matter. Where were you? And Peter and Cindy? Where on earth are they?"

"Oh, out on the deck," said Jan, reddening. "We kind of peeked into the lifeboats."

"All this time?" her mother asked, surprised.

"Yes. Where's Greg and Marcia?" Jan asked as casually as she dared. She felt she ought to tell her parents more, but Greg should be the one to decide how much to reveal. He was really the leader of the group.

Suddenly her eyes caught sight of Oscar and Mary as they re-entered the room. They actually had the colossal gall to come back to the party, she thought indignantly. Didn't it occur to them that they might have been missed in all this time? But then she remembered that she and Bobby had been gone a long while too.

Now Mr. and Mrs. Bailey were moving in on them and they were actually bringing along Mary and Oscar!

"I want you to meet some business associates of ours," Mr. Bailey said jovially. "This is Mary Rogers, who is one of our finest jewelry designers, and Mr. Oscar Remak, one of Los Angeles' most important jewelers."

Jan did a quick double take in her head. A designer of jewelry and a man who sold jewelry. It made a lot of sense, Jan told herself. They wanted to sell the stolen jewels! Probably to some character who was a crook just like them. Oh how she longed to speak up and say what she thought. Right in front of them all.

"Look. I know exactly what you two crooks are up to," Jan pictured herself declaring in a loud, angry tone. "I'm going right up to the captain this very minute and tell him just what I heard in the lifeboat. I'll tell him all about your alternate plan and what you're going to do at the big gala party and all."

She imagined the look on Oscar's fat face. His big dog's eyes would roll in absolute agony as he heard her words. Out would come the yellow silk handkerchief from the pocket of his white jacket and he would wipe his sweating face. And as for Mary Rogers, her face would go dead white and her hand would fly to her throat.

"Oh no . . . no," she would protest. "You're mistaken. It wasn't us. . . . I know it wasn't us you heard by those funnels."

"Who was it then, I'd like to know? A couple of ghosts?" Jan would reply bitterly. "Look, I was there and so was my brother Bobby Brady and I'll get him to tell you himself. If I can pull him away from all those idiotic foods and stop him from stuffing his face with nuts and shrimp and everything he can get his fists on."

She was enjoying her thoughts of Oscar and Mary's embarrassment so much that she failed to see her brother Greg waving to her from the other side of the room. Her father gently patted her shoulder and told her that Greg wanted to talk to her. She blinked her eyes, said goodbye politely to Oscar, Mary, and the Baileys and moved over to Greg's side.

"Hey come on!" he said anxiously. "What did you find out anyhow?"

"I didn't think you really cared one way or the other, Big Brother," Jan said, wanting to tease him a little. "You were so completely wrapped up in Miss Universe of 1982."

"Oh cut that out," Greg said. "Tell me."

"We got to talk. I heard all about their plans. Big plans," Jan said.

His eyes lit up with surprise. "You did? Wow. Hey, we got to call a special Council of War. This calls for it."

"When?" Jan asked excitedly.

"As soon as possible." He thought for a moment. Then he snapped his fingers. "I got it. Right after dinner we get all the kids and say we want to look at the sunset on the other side of the ship. Then we can be alone and discuss our next moves. Okay?"

"Great!" Jan said.

"Okay you tell the kids. I'll take care of Marcia."

"Where is she?" Jan wanted to know.

"Well, we're all outside sitting on some deck chairs, having a kind of get-acquainted party of our own. I just came in to get us some more nuts and candy." He looked uncomfortable as his sister smiled at him.

"Look, when you get a little older you'll understand these things a lot better," he said, not looking at her in the eyes.

"Yes, I guess I will," she said, glowering at him, "but I hope I don't act as silly as you're acting right now over a girl!"

Greg's jaw hardened as he fought not to answer back.

"Look, we'll meet on the top deck near the

front of the ship right after dinner. And we walk out one at a time so nobody notices anything."

Then he swung on his heel and turned away before Jan could launch any more peppery remarks.

The Brady kids were unusually silent during the meal that followed. When Mike or Carol Brady tried to ask them anything, they either looked up blankly or answered very briefly. Even Alice was puzzled by their behavior.

"Hey, what's got into you kids anyhow?" she asked. "By this time you should have started at least a dozen fights here. I expected Jan and Peter to argue which dessert is better, Bobby and Cindy to fight over how far we're from Los Angeles, and Marcia to find fault with what Greg said about the uniforms on the crew. Or lots of other things. I thought you'd all be excited about the party and meeting Doris and Harry Bailey.

"I don't understand it. Aren't you excited over meeting your old schoolmates on the ship? Didn't the party give you a boost?"

"They weren't there half the time," Carol noted.

"More than that," Mike put in. "They just popped in and then popped out. I hardly saw them at all. Except Bobby, who attacked a whip-cream cake as if he were starving to death."

The Brady kids, however, said nothing. They were too excited about their secrets and they couldn't wait till the meal was finished so they could go outside and talk about their next moves in the Great Jewel Robbery. They were so eager to leave, in fact, that they didn't even bother to order second helpings of the rich dessert, a delicious concoction made with chocolate, cherries, nuts, ice cream, and whipped cream.

"Hey, you mean you're not having seconds on this?" Alice asked, thunderstruck by their lack of interest.

"You can have our second portions, Alice dear," Marcia said as she left. The others followed her at two-minute intervals, with the casual excuse that they wanted to stroll around the deck or look at the sunset.

When they had all left, the three adults looked at one another, completely puzzled.

"Did you ever see anything like that?" Carol asked. "I thought they'd devour those second helpings of dessert like hungry wolves. I hope they aren't getting seasick or anything like that. I don't know what to do. Ask them or just wait and see if this goes on like this. It's very strange."

"Well, I know what I'm going to do," Mike Brady said. "I'm going to eat one of their second portions."

"But their leaving like that," Carol said, disturbed. "Their silence. They're acting like some secret agents on a mission who want to keep from revealing anything. Doesn't that disturb you, Mike?"

"Oh, they're probably running around the deck playing tag or hide-and-seek," Mike said, laughing. "I'm sure they've forgotten that silly jewel robbery story by now."

He was wrong. They were not running. They

were seated in a circle in a group of chairs near the bow of the vessel and speaking very quietly and determinedly.

"Okay, guys," Greg said carefully. "We have to decide what our next move is. It's pretty clear they're getting ready to pull something very soon."

"I say let's tell the captain," Marcia put in. "He seems to be pretty intelligent."

"I think we ought to tell Mom and Daddy and Alice," Cindy offered timidly.

Greg shook his head. "Not yet. Look, I think the grown-ups think we're just imagining at least ninety percent of this whole thing."

"But we heard Oscar and Mary talk about it," Jan protested. "Didn't we, Bobby?"

"Right," Bobby said. "He said it all very clearly. We could hear every word."

"So what?" Peter interrupted. "All he says to the captain is that you're nuts. That you just imagined it. And besides you'll have to say you hid in the lifeboat. You're not supposed to do that, Bobby."

Greg shook his head. "Too bad Peter wasn't there with his little tape recorder, so we could have got it down word for word. Then we could play it back for the captain and he'd know we weren't lying."

"I could try to do that later. Follow them around till they speak about the robbery again," Peter suggested.

"Yeah but who knows when they'll give you another chance," Greg groaned. "Anyway that's neither here nor there. We have to do something positive now. I think the best thing to do now is to keep as close tabs on this mob as possible. Till we get the goods on them. We need evidence that will convince the captain and purser. Your idea about following them around with a tape recorder is a good one but we need more than one machine working for us."

"What do you mean?" Peter asked. "If we have their words on one tape, that's all we need isn't it?"

"So what happens if you're not there when they talk," Greg said, annoyed. "Obviously we have to get more machines."

"How?" Jan asked.

They thought hard for a moment and then Marcia laughed and clapped her hands in triumph as the idea came to her.

"I have it. Look, we can't use our money to buy food or the usual things on board. But there's a store inside. On one of the lower decks with all kinds of things. And I think I saw a small tape recorder down there. We can get several."

Greg thought for a while and nodded. "That's good, Marcia, but I don't think we can get five recorders. It would look very funny if we all went for the same thing."

"That's right," Peter put in. "Everybody'd get suspicious right away. We never do that at home. Mom and Dad and Alice would start wondering what it was all about."

"Yeah, but worse than that," Jan said, "the crooks would wonder what we're up to. I mean, remember they've got contacts in the crew. People who are ready to tell them everything. Well, suppose one of these guys pops over to them and says all the kids are buying tape machines. Right off they'll be on their guard against us."

"She's right," Bobby said. "None of us'll be able to get near them with a recorder. It'll all be wasted and we'll buy all that stuff for nothing."

"Okay," Greg said quickly. "We can't all buy tape machines. What we'll do is buy one more and keep both of them working at all times. When we follow Mary or Lakey or the other guys, whoever is watching them carries a tape recorder. We got to get it all down on tape so they believe us."

They listened carefully as Jan and Bobby repeated what Mary and Oscar had discussed near the ship's funnels.

"Whew!" Cindy said. "Can you imagine how fantastic all that would sound if we'd got in on the tape recorder."

The information about the crooks' friend or friends on the ship's staff was especially interesting to Greg.

"We got to find out who they are," he said. "That's terribly important. We can follow them and take pictures of them once we know their identities. Peter, you have your camera ready to shoot at all times. Make sure there's good fast film in the camera."

"That's not fast enough," Peter said. "It'll take some time for the pictures to be developed. If we want to nail these guys down, we ought to have the pictures right away to show the captain or the purser."

"Right," Greg agreed. "If we can show Oscar or Lakey or any of the others in a huddle with a steward, it'll show them later that they were in cahoots. They were planning the robbery together."

"Not necessarily," Marcia intervened. "It would depend on what they said to one another. That's why we need the tape recorders handy."

"They'll have to be small too and easily hidden," Peter noted. "If we carry them around too openly or on big straps, that gives it all away."

"The one I saw was pretty small," Marcia said. "But I don't think any of us ought to buy it. Who can we get?"

"How about Mom or Dad?" Cindy inquired.

Greg shook his head. "I think Alice is a better choice. But we need a faster camera too." He looked at Marcia, who seemed to be lost in a reverie. "Something occur to you, Marcia?"

She blushed a little. "Well, I just remembered that Harry Bailey has a Polaroid camera. His dad gave it to him for coming up with a straight 'A' record last semester."

"Maybe you could borrow it," Greg said quickly.

"Hey, that's exactly what we need," Peter threw in. "With a Polaroid you could have the finished picture right after you take it. Come on, Marcia, ask him for it. Just tell him you need it for a while."

"Yes but how long, Peter?" she asked, "I can't expect him to lend it to me for the whole trip." She turned to Greg. "Hey, I just remembered. Harry told me that his sister has one too. For her birthday. Only she doesn't use it much. She hasn't much interest in taking pictures, it seems."

"Well that settles that," Peter said. "We get Alice to buy the recorder and we get our two lovebirds to ask their sweethearts to give them their cameras."

"You'd better watch that fat mouth of yours, Peter," Marcia said, "or I may just stuff that camera down your dumb throat."

Greg was also pained by Peter's remark, but he had too many other things to think about to complain now.

"Okay enough of that, guys. We got to work fast. Now listen carefully while I work out a schedule. A team of two people will be following each pair of crooks from now on until they go into their cabins."

"You mean all the time?" Cindy said, her eyes widening.

"All the time," Greg said firmly. "We can't take chances on missing what they say or who they meet. They're liable to meet their accomplices on the crew at any old time. Some of us better be along to catch it whether it's before our bedtime or afterwards.

"There's too much at stake."

"What's a stakeout, by the way?" Cindy wanted to know. Peter and Greg exchanged glances of surprise and disbelief.

66

"You mean you never heard of a stakeout?" Peter asked.

"Oh she's just a baby," Bobby said, laughing. "How do you expect her to know anything like that?"

"I'm not a baby!" Cindy snapped back at him "I just don't know. Do you know, smarty? If you know so much, why don't you tell me?"

Bobby looked uncomfortable but said nothing.

Greg patiently explained to Cindy that a stakeout meant that detectives simply shadowed some suspects, following them everywhere and making notes on what they said and did.

"We'll keep after them until they spill the beans and let us know what their other plan is."

Two days later their careful stakeouts of the crooks told them exactly what the alternative plan was. It was so clever that it took them all by surprise.

Chapter SEVEN

The information came to them unexpectedly and they would not have realized what they had except for the luck of having the tape recorders handy.

It had been a little difficult getting Alice to

buy the second tape machine without blabbing about the whole thing to Mike and Carol Brady. First of all they did not have quite enough money to buy it. It had cost more than they expected, more than it would at home, because everything cost more on the boat.

So they had to ask Alice for a loan, since even after they pooled all their saved-up allowances, they were still nowhere close to the price. The only other way would have been to appeal to Mike and they decided that would mean answering too many questions. But Alice had some too.

"But why do you want the darn thing?" she asked. "You already got one. Peter's. What's the whole point of getting another?"

Greg had smiled and told her it was a birthday gift for Mike whose birth date would come soon after they got back.

Alice looked at him for a minute, then shrugged her shoulders and nodded.

"Under the circumstances," she smiled. "I'll not only get it, but I'll add my own contribution, too. You won't have to borrow anything. I'll make up the difference between what you already have and the purchase price. Okay?"

The kids looked conscience-stricken. They felt badly about having to lie to Alice about the reason for the purchase. But if that wasn't bad enough, taking her money under false pretenses was worse. Greg stepped forward, cleared his throat as if he were about to make a momentous announcement, and said it was out of the question for them to take her money.

"This is just from us kids—you know. No offense meant, Alice. We all love you and we're grateful. But we'd feel better if we did it ourselves. You understand, don't you?"

Alice grinned. "Sure. I get it. You want to keep it strictly among yourselves. Okay. I think that makes the gift a better one. Mike will appreciate it even more. I'll be glad to loan you the money."

Half an hour later Alice had purchased the recorder and given it to them. It was a small machine and was carried in a case. To most observers it would look like a camera, which is exactly what the kids had hoped.

The two tape machines were always with them; ready for duty. Peter's or the new one was carried by whichever one of them was on the stakeout. The Brady kids all took turns. Each team of two was on duty for two hours and then had some time off. All day long the conspirators were being watched.

The watches began at breakfast time and someone was near the crooks at all times. When they were strolling on deck, eating their meals, or even sitting in their cabins.

If the woman went to the beauty parlor to have her hair done, then Marcia and Jan or Jan and Cindy would go along to listen to her conversation. Similarly, the boys visited the steamroom and the gymnasium when the male crooks went there.

For a long while they drew blanks. They were eager to find out which women would be hit with robberies and what the alternate plan was.

But nothing was happening. Their tape recorders merely registered talk that had nothing to do with the robbery. Then late one afternoon, the kids scored beautifully.

It was totally unexpected. Marcia discovered that Mary was due for another hairdressing session. She had already been to the first, only to listen to a lot of drivel about movies and clothes as Mary chatted amiably with the female hairdresser. She was so disgusted that she nearly gave up but she still hung on in the vain hope that maybe the girl doing Mary's hair was her contact on the staff.

The next afternoon, shortly before lunchtime, Mary came back for another hair job. Some male hairdresser did her hair this time. Unlike the earlier session, there was no one else in the place. Marcia and Cindy entered, then changed their minds about staying. It would be too obvious that they were watching Mary if they came back every time she was there. Instead they waited till the girl was placed in a closed-off booth where a large hair drier was turned on.

Marcia and Cindy waited till the hairdresser left for a few minutes and then sneaked into the adjoining booth. Working quickly, Marcia turned on the new machine and directed the microphone toward Mary's booth. For what seemed hours, nothing happened. Then they heard voices and what the voices said was indeed quite interesting.

"Hi," a new voice, a female voice said. "Can we talk?"

"I guess so," Mary said quietly. "Arthur's left. He'll be out for a while. I think he went to get some new towels and other stuff. Are you all set?"

"Absolutely. The minute we enter the canal, we'll go to work," said the newcomer.

"You've taken all the precautions necessary?" Mary inquired. "I mean, it would be awful if you were interrupted by anything or anyone. We can't stand any surprises with this operation."

The other girl laughed. "No trouble. The canal is the best time to pull the job. It'd be very bad if we were surprised. I'd lose my job. They'd put me off in Puerto Rico. And Helen too. But we know what we're doing. I'm counting on the rest of you to keep the old biddy pretty busy. I don't want her to go back to her room."

"How much time will you need to get all the jewels?" Mary asked quietly.

"I guess thirty or forty minutes. An hour at the outside if Helen or I have to fool around with locks on her suitcases. I'm still not sure who'll be in there. Helen or me."

"You'll have the full hour," Mary promised. "Are you sure you picked the best girl to rob?"

"No doubt about it. She's the richest one of the six we listed with a lot of diamonds and she's terribly absent-minded. She left a diamond bracelet in the beauty parlor a couple of days ago and Arturo had to run over to me to give it back."

"Okay," Mary said firmly. "She's the right target then. What I want, what Oscar and Lakey and Harry all want, in fact, is something that will distract everyone. See, we're eager to make it look as if two jewel gangs are out working the ship. One gang is working the cabins—sort of an inside job, you might say. The other will make a stab at robbing the women during the gala. If we're lucky, we can pull off both deals."

"But why take a chance on two deals?" the woman talking to Mary asked. "Wouldn't it be better to work just one and try to make it a big haul."

"Yes it would," Mary replied. "Except for one thing. We may be under surveillance because those Brady kids snitched what they heard in their cabin. From Lakey and Harry. But there's still another reason, an important reason."

"What's that?" the other woman asked, puzzled.

"Simple. Some of the women are cautious about keeping expensive jewelry in their cabins. They've put it under lock and key in the purser's office."

"No!" the woman said, expressing strong annoyance. "Not after we've worked so hard to set this thing up. Not after all the chances we took. You realize how many people have risked their jobs in this deal?"

"I'm quite aware of it," Mary said.

"Yeah, well now you tell me they're keeping their ice in the ship's safe. What are we supposed to do? Blow the safe?"

"Take it easy," Mary said soothingly. "The woman you're robbing isn't one of the worriers. She's kept plenty of jewels in her cabin. All I meant was that we'll have to wait till the captain holds his big gala party to flush them out of hiding. That's when all the rich biddies get their big jewels out of safekeeping. They come to the party dressed to kill. They want to show off. You know what I mean."

The other girl laughed understandingly. "I dig what you mean. We get two shots at the jewels that way. We may get the bulk of the stuff, in fact."

"That's it," Mary crowed. "By the time this ship pulls into San Juan, Puerto Rico, we'll have over half a million dollars' worth of jewels."

"Very good," the other woman said. "And in Puerto Rico? What happens there?"

The outside door opened suddenly and Mary told her companion to lower her voice.

"I can't talk anymore. Arturo's got a big pair of ears. We'll finish it up later. Just warn the others to be ready to move when Lakey or I or Oscar give the signal. Okay?"

"Got you, dear. Good luck to you."

"Good luck to all of us," Mary corrected.

As soon as they could escape quietly from the beauty parlor, Marcia and Cindy made their way to their brothers' cabin. The news they gave the boys excited them all.

"Great," Greg said as they listened to the playback of the conversation on tape. "Now we know they're planning something when we enter the canal."

"What canal is that?" Bobby asked innocently.

73

"The Panama Canal, dum-dum," Peter snorted. "Don't you know any geography, for heaven's sake?"

"We haven't got to that yet in our geography class," Bobby apologized. "Is it a big one, the Panama Canal I mean?"

"Big?" Marcia cried. "It's gigantic. It takes hours and hours to get through. You go through all sorts of rugged terrain as you move from the Pacific to the Atlantic."

"You do?" Peter nodded knowingly, ignoring the look of complete wonderment on his younger brother's face.

"I had no idea there was such a big canal there," Bobby said. "It must be fabulous to look at. You mean it actually goes from the Atlantic to the Pacific ocean?"

"That's right," Greg said. "It was built to save people the need to sail all the way around South America. I mean you used to take weeks longer to get to Europe from California under the old conditions."

"Wow," Bobby said. "I'm looking forward to seeing that."

"We all are," Peter said. "Outside of maybe the Suez Canal over in Africa, the Panama Canal is probably the biggest ditch in the whole world."

The description of the canal made them all so curious that everyone in the room was full of questions about it. How long was it, when was it built, how deep was the water in it, and more. Till Greg pounded on the bulkhead wall with his fist and told them to stop.

"Come on, you guys, this isn't a class in geography. We're having a War Council on how to stop a bunch of smart crooks from making a giant heist. Now let's get down to that, okay?"

They all listened silently and obediently to their chief.

"Okay, let's take what we know, one thing at a time," Greg said, summing up for them. "We know now that there are at least five crooks on the ship working as a kind of gang: Lakey, Harry, Oscar, Mary, the woman in the beauty parlor with her today, and a member of the crew called Helen. Right?"

"What about Arturo?" Marcia put in. "He's in it with them, isn't he?"

"I don't think so, Marcia," Greg said carefully. "If he were in it, why would Mary tell her friend to hush up because he has big ears?"

"That's right," Cindy said. "She was worried he might overhear what they were talking about."

"Look, the first thing we have to find out," Peter said, "is who this mysterious Helen is."

"And who is the woman they're planning to rob when the ship enters the canal tomorrow," Greg pointed out. "Too bad you didn't hear her name, Marcia," he added. "If we knew who she was, we could watch her cabin and try to catch the crooks red-handed."

"I got an idea," Peter said suddenly. "Why don't we find out who Helen is and watch her movements. We know she's probably going to go after the lady's jewels. We aren't really sure that Lakey, Mary, Oscar, or Harry are."

75

"He's right," Marcia said excitedly. "They're too vulnerable to take a chance like breaking into a stateroom or trying to sneak into it. Much better to let one of the chambermaids or stewards do it. The people who work in the passengers' rooms regularly."

"Okay," Greg said. "Let's all make inquiries about Helen. Only it can't be too obvious. We need an excuse to ask about her."

"How about if we say we found something of hers," Cindy asked.

"Like what?" Bobby wanted to know. "A pillow?"

"No, silly," his sister responded. "Maybe she lost her purse or her compact. With her name on it."

"No," Greg said thoughtfully, "then the people might wonder why we didn't turn these things into the lost-and-found. No, it has to be more discreet, less open to suspicion."

They racked their brains for a minute silently. Then Jan came up with an idea. "Know what might work? Suppose we say that we met Helen's cousin back home and she asked us to look her up and give her a message. How about that? We'd have to give it to her ourselves."

Greg patted his sister affectionately. "Good thinking, Jan. Good thinking. That's what we do. Okay, we meet back here in an hour and see what we've come up with."

They separated and each of the kids moved to another part of the ship and asked various members of the crew the same question. They followed Greg's advice and acted as casual as they could.

The first few questions drew zero. The ship's crew was larger than they had imagined. Not everyone knew every other member of the staff.

Cindy was the one who struck gold, though, with her query. When she asked her third person, a man swabbing the deck, he scratched his forehead and said, "I think she's a maid on B deck some place. I remember somebody named Helen asked me to bring some cart over to wheel away some dirty bedclothes a couple of mornings ago."

Immediately Cindy got hold of Marcia and together the sisters walked through the halls of B deck. They walked slowly until they met a middle-aged maid who was carrying an armful of towels.

"Oh excuse me, miss," Marcia asked. "Did you see Helen? We'd like to give her a message from friends of hers back home."

"Sure," the woman replied promptly. Try Cabin B-17. I think she's making the beds there." Then she eyed them somewhat quizzically. "You're not on B deck, are you? I don't remember seeing you."

"We changed our room," Cindy popped in, paying no attention to her sister's warning nudge with her foot. The maid nodded slowly and then, giving them another look, asked if they wanted her to call Helen out to talk to them.

"Er no, no," Marcia said embarrassedly. "We're going that way anyway, so we'll just look into B-17."

They walked away quickly, avoiding the maid's puzzled eyes. Halfway down the corridor they realized the numbers of the rooms were going the wrong way and changed their course to go back. As they reached the cabin marked B-17, the door was slightly ajar. They peeked in and looked to see who was inside.

Making the beds in the large cabin was a very pretty, young redheaded girl in her middle twenties. Her face was freckled and she had a small upturned nose and eyes of a deep blue color. They watched her for a minute, both feeling very exhilarated that they had found her. Then Marcia pulled her sister away. When they were safely on the deck above, they spoke excitedly.

"All we have to do now is watch her," Marcia said. "As soon as she moves to some other cabin, off B deck, then we'll know she's after the jewels."

"How do you know it isn't a cabin on B deck where she works?" Cindy asked. "If that's where she's going to steal the lady's jewels, we can't tell till she's finished because she's got a reason to work in those cabins."

"I'll tell you why, little sister," Marcia said, smiling. "Because the lady who's going to be robbed is very rich and probably has a cabin on the most expensive deck of the ship, the top one. I know that's the one because Daddy said it was too rich for his blood. Only millionaires lived on it."

"You ought to be a detective," Cindy said, laughing. "What do we do now, Marcia?"

"That's easy," Marcia said. "We keep careful tabs on little Miss Helen all through the Panama Canal."

"That's not fair," Cindy said. "I wanted to see the Canal."

"You will, dear. But one of us has to watch Helen all the time. We'll take turns watching her."

Cindy nodded happily.

What she didn't know was that the jewel thieves were going to take turns watching them. Shortly after the girls had asked for Helen, the maid to whom they had spoken, entered B-17.

"Did you see a couple of young kids come in here just now, Helen?" she asked.

"Young kids?" Helen's eyebrows wrinkled. "No. Who were they?"

"Don't know, but they acted kind of funny so I watched them. First they walked the wrong way, then they doubled back and peeked in here. I saw them give you the once-over and then scram up to the next deck. What's it all about?"

"I haven't the slightest idea," Helen answered smoothly. "Must have been some mistake. Maybe they meant someone else."

Her outer smoothness hid her inner turmoil. As soon as the other maid had spoken, she felt her knees grow weak.

No sooner had the woman turned away than she phoned Lakey's cabin.

"Listen, this is——"

"No names," he barked. "What is it?"

"I got to talk to you personally. Right away."

"I told you never to call unless there's a real

emergency," Lakey shouted. "You're taking a big risk when you call."

"This is a big emergency. I got to talk to you right now. It's very urgent."

There was a pause. Then Lakey told her to come up as soon as she could make it. "Not here. Mary's room."

When she arrived at Mary's cabin ten minutes later, she found them all gathered there waiting impatiently. For a moment, her knees still quaking, she studied Oscar, Mary, Lakey, and Harry.

"All right," Lakey said tersely. "Spill it. What is it that's so important?"

Chapter EIGHT

Helen slowly told them about the inquiries made by Marcia and Cindy and their strange movements in the vicinity of the room she was working in.

"Son of a gun," Mary said, annoyed. "How'd they find out?" She thought about it for a moment. "Wait a minute, they might have followed me into the beauty salon and eavesdropped. I was talking about Helen . . . but I thought we were alone."

"Are you certain?" Lakey asked harshly. "You

sure you didn't blab about Helen when you were talking to Oscar the time the ratty kids were spying on you?"

"I swear I didn't," Mary protested.

"Do they know about the other people working for us on the boat?" Lakey demanded.

"No," Mary said slowly.

"Are you sure" he shouted, "that you didn't blab their names to little Eve while those dumb brats were spying on you in the beauty salon?"

"She didn't, Lakey," Helen chimed in. "I know she didn't. Eve would have told me." Lakey ignored her.

"How about the Sanderson dame?" Lakey said in a sneering voice, "how many times did you mention her?"

"Lakey, you gotta believe me," Mary pleaded. "I didn't mention Sanderson at all. Not once. I started, but then I think Arturo came back. Anyway, I heard a noise and that put me on my guard."

"You think, you don't know?"

"My guess is she's right," Helen said. "Arturo never stays out too long. Anyway she didn't mention Mrs. Sanderson."

"That's nice," Oscar said jeeringly. "At least we won't expect the purser or the captain to greet us when we try to steal the jewels in her stateroom."

"But they know Helen's going to be involved, so they'll be watching her," Harry said. "There's only one thing to do. Take Helen off it. Otherwise, if they're spying on her, they'll be right be-

81

hind her when she enters the Sanderson cabin."

"Can't do that!" Lakey said. "She's the only one of us who wouldn't be suspected if somebody barges in. Even if the Sanderson dame herself came in. Helen can always say she's substituting for the regular maid."

"But the kids know who she is," Harry protested. "They'll interfere with the whole thing. They know what she's up to."

Lakey thought for a moment. "You got a point there. There's only one thing to do. We got to stop the kids cold."

"How?" Oscar said, interestedly.

"I'll figure out a way," Lakey said mysteriously. "I got a whole day to think about it."

The Brady kids could barely shut their eyes that night. The ship was supposed to enter the Panama Canal immediately after breakfast that next morning. Peter spent what seemed like hours to his brothers checking to see that the camera worked properly. He was so nervous about touching it, in fact, that when Bobby accidentally fingered it, he screamed that Bobby would "ruin it" before he could shoot one picture of the canal.

Greg and Marcia, meanwhile, had gone to the ship's library and come back with several books and pamphlets about the incredible engineering marvel they were about to see.

After dinner Greg read some facts about the canal to his brothers and sisters. Ever since the days of the early Spanish conquerors, there had been plans to divide North and South America somewhere near the present canal. Hernando Cortes, who defeated Montezuma, the great Aztec emperor of ancient Mexico, had first come up with the idea.

"You see, they were trying to find a new sea route to India," Greg explained. "Everybody in Europe wanted to get to India and the Spice Islands."

"What are the Spice Islands?" Cindy asked.

"Places like Moluccas near Indonesia," Greg said, "where they grow pepper and other spices. In the early days, according to historians, Europeans had had to have plenty of spices or their meat would spoil. They had to salt a lot of it to keep it even a few weeks, but that wasn't enough. Other spices were required to keep the meat fresh over a longer period of time."

Cindy continued to interrupt her big brother as he quoted from the history book.

"But that doesn't make sense, Greg," she protested. "How could they eat meat full of pepper. It's impossible!"

"It's not impossible, Cindy," Greg said patiently. "The book says it made the meat much tastier. In fact, according to the same author, the ancient Romans loved to put pepper on sweet things too. They just loved the taste of the stuff."

"But I still don't see how——" Cindy began.

"Let him read more about the Panama Canal," said Jan irritably. "We're getting off the subject. I want to learn about the canal since we're going to go through it tomorrow."

Greg began again. "Well, the book says the

French tried to make a canal during the nineteenth century, across the Isthmus of Panama—that's the narrowest part of Central America, south of Mexico. But they failed because of the engineering difficulties and because of the Yellow Fever epidemics. The place was mostly jungle and full of mosquitos. Then they sent down a team of marines and tried an experiment with a new serum that beat the disease. After that they could go ahead and it was finished in 1914."

"How big is it?" Peter wanted to know.

"Well, it's nearly fifty miles from one ocean to the other," Greg said. "They used a lot of existing rivers and lakes but it wasn't enough. They still had to create special dams and artificial lakes to get the ships through from one side to the other. And locks."

"Locks?" Bobby said, puzzled. "What kind of locks? You mean they locked up the ships?"

"No," Greg smiled. "Let's see if I can explain it to you. The book's a little too complicated. You see, the Atlantic and Pacific oceans are at different levels. You can't go straight from one ocean to another, the way you can in the Suez Canal. There you have a level canal—it's almost like crossing one side of a big lake to another.

"But in Panama it's mountainous. You've got lakes and rivers at different levels. Sometimes there's as much as eighty-five feet difference. To get you from one lake level to the next body of water, for example, they put the ship into a lock. What it is is a kind of big tub with gates. The ship goes into this tub and then the gates are closed.

"Once that happens the engineers let water go in or they let it out in order to either raise the ship to another level or get it down to a lower level."

"How do the ships move through the lock?" Marcia asked, fascinated by the explanation.

"They have electric locomotives pulling them through," Greg told her. "You'll probably see it all tomorrow."

"Unless I'm chasing our little jewel thief, Helen," she said glumly.

"Oh, heck, it takes seven or eight hours to get from the Pacific Ocean to the Atlantic," Greg said. "You won't chase her that long."

"You want to bet," Marcia said, looking very serious. "I got a feeling about little old Helen. She's going to be harder to track down than a drunken monkey. And I think I'm going to need a lot of help. So don't you guys get too wrapped up in that big ditch."

Marcia's fears made them laugh but they were well-founded. As soon as breakfast was finished, Marcia and Cindy gloomily went in search of Helen while the other Bradys crowded the rails of the ship. They were entering the canal just as Mike Brady finished his second cup of coffee.

"Come on, gang," he cried, as he saw the locks approach through the window. "This is a historic moment—the first Brady trip across the Panama Canal."

He and Carol looked astonished as first Cindy

and Marcia excused themselves and then Jan and Peter.

"Where are you guys going?" Mike said. "Don't you want to see this thing? We're going through the Panama Canal for heaven's sake!"

"I know, Dad," Peter said uncomfortably. Marcia, Cindy, and Jan smiled sickly grins at their father.

"I don't understand you?" Carol Brady said. "Aren't you excited? I talked to the Baileys about the canal and they said Doris and Harry could hardly sleep for fear they'd miss it."

"I couldn't sleep either, Mom," Cindy said quickly. "That's all I could think about and Greg told us all about it. About the locks and the lifting of the ships and everything."

"Then why aren't you all crowding the ship's rails like everybody else?" Mike Brady asked in an exasperated tone.

"I think they must be sick, Mr. Brady," Alice said, pressing her lips together. "If you ask me, they've been acting a little touched ever since the Bailey shindig. All that running in and out . . ."

"Are you sick, children?" Mike asked with concern in his voice.

"No, Dad," Peter said quickly. "We're just trying to see who can make it around the deck first going in opposite directions. Right, guys?"

The other kids all nodded, while avoiding their father's eyes.

Mike, Carol, and Alice looked absolutely dumbfounded. "You mean you prefer racing around the deck that way to seeing one of man's greatest engineering marvels? One of the great wonders of the world?"

There was a deep silence and Alice looked them over once and snorted. "I told you they were touched!"

"We'd better start moving, gang," Peter said uneasily. "Take some good pictures with your movie camera, Dad. I want to see what we missed later."

They shot a smile at Greg and Bobby, who were staying behind, and moved away, trying hard to overlook the amazed stares of Alice, Mike, and Carol.

"I'm really worried about them," Carol said. "You don't think they're still chasing around after jewel thieves, do you, Mike?"

Mike laughed. "No, I talked to the captain about that. He said kids often make up stories like that on board ship. Or else they distort things they think they heard. No, I just think the ship has had a wild effect on them; they'll probably calm down as soon as we touch land. I've seen a lot of other kids racing around, too. Come on, let's see the canal."

It took Cindy and Marcia ten minutes to find Helen. She was finishing a room on B deck. Since the door was wide open, they could see her clearly from their hiding place across the corridor. If she were preparing to rob anyone, she gave no signs of it.

"Hey, I hope we don't have to stand here all day," Marcia said after half an hour's waiting.

"And I'm just dying to see the ship get lifted through all those locks, aren't you?"

"Yes," Cindy said, but her face turned very serious. "But we can't. We promised Greg and Peter and Jan and Bobby in the War Council that we'd never leave our post. Just like Jan and Peter promised to follow Lakey and Harry."

"Yeah but . . ." Marcia made a face. "Oh well, it's only for two hours, then we'll be relieved by Greg and Bobby and we can watch the canal—if there's anything left to see by then. With our luck we'll be all through it by then."

"But it takes a long time Marcia, hours and hours, right?"

Marcia, keeping one eye on Helen, turned to answer her little sister. As she looked behind Cindy, her eyes widened with astonishment. Coming down the corridor was Harry Bailey, smiling broadly.

What was he doing here? And now when she had to keep watch on Helen? Perhaps he was just passing through the corridor.

"Hey, Marcia," he cried, obviously delighted to see her. "How goes?" He beamed at Cindy, who gave him a cool, rather annoyed stare. He seemed totally unaware that he had interfered in anything.

"Hi, Harry," Marcia said apprehensively. "You on your way to something big? It looks like it from that grin on your face." She tried to lighten her tone, so he would not see how tensed up she was.

"Why no," Harry answered, surprised at her question. "I was looking for you."

"For me?" Marcia said disbelievingly. Helen had finished the room and now had emerged from the door. Her arms were laden with towels and pillow cases and she was marching away from them!

"Yes," Harry said. "Look, I wanted to ask you if you'd like to play shuffleboard with me a little later. They're having a tournament for junior passengers on board—doubles. Two people on each side. If a couple win, they get a special silver cup—I mean two of them, with the ship's insignia."

Marcia looked as if she were going to be sick. Helen, the jewel thief, was running away from her while Harry was drooling about a shuffleboard tournament.

"Hey, Marcia I think we'd better go," Cindy said warningly. She looked at Harry as if she wished to kick him in the shins. Without waiting for a word from Marcia, she tugged at her sister's arm and pulled her in the direction that Helen had gone. Marcia, in a proper dilemma as to whether to stay and talk to Harry or run after Helen, let herself be pulled away finally.

To her astonishment Harry Bailey was walking with her!

"I—I'm in a hurry, Harry," Marcia said lamely.

"Where you going?" he asked pleasantly as they turned the corner.

"No place," Cindy declared loudly. "We just want to take a walk, that's all."

Oh no, Cindy, Marcia said to herself. I wish you hadn't said that.

"Oh well I'll walk with you. I've been wanting to talk to you, Marcia. About the junior prom."

The junior prom! Marcia's heart nearly leaped to her mouth. He was asking her about the junior prom? Did that mean he wanted her to go with him!

"Look, excuse us, Harry," Cindy said, breaking into Marcia's thoughts. "I gotta talk to my sister a second."

"Sure," Harry said. He lingered behind them. Cindy pressed Marcia against the wall and spoke into her ear.

"Listen, we gotta get away from that pest."

"He's not a pest!" Marcia protested. "He's very nice."

"Yeah? Maybe he's too nice," Cindy said, giving Harry Bailey a scowl. "What's he doing here?"

"What do you mean?"

"How come he shows up on B deck just when we're watching Helen?" Cindy asked gravely. "Isn't that funny?"

"Why?" Marcia said. "Maybe he just happened to be looking for me on B deck."

"Yeah? And he just happens to walk here at the second she's ready to walk out of the room? That's very funny, isn't it, Marcia?"

"I don't think so," Marcia said. But she did not sound very convincing even to herself.

"Say goodbye to him quick or we'll lose her," hissed Cindy.

When Marcia, unwilling to offend him, said nothing, Cindy took the initiative.

"I'm sorry, Harry, we got an urgent appointment at the doctor's. Marcia doesn't feel well."

Before Harry, who was standing there with his mouth wide open, could say a single word, Cindy had pulled her sister around the next corner. Out of his sight and hearing.

"Why on earth did you tell him that?" Marcia said, infuriated with Cindy. "Now he won't ask me to the junior prom. Are you crazy or something?"

"I was just trying to stay with Helen before she gave us the slip," Cindy said. Then she sighed.

"Well, it doesn't matter now. She's probably in the woman's apartment now, stealing everything she's got."

Helen was nowhere to be seen.

"I just hope Jan and Peter have picked up her trail," Cindy said disgustedly. "Or at least Lakey and Harry."

Jan and Peter had found Lakey and Harry near the shuffleboard courts and for a long time were very pleased with themselves. They could watch the crooks and the canal activity at the same time.

They saw hordes of men running on both sides of the canal, pulling at machinery, hoisting cranes and booms and shouting orders to one another in English and Spanish. From time to time Jan and Peter would turn to see if Lakey and Harry were still occupied with their game. They did, indeed, seem to be thoroughly engrossed in it. They seemed totally oblivious to what was happening in the canal locks or the lovely jungle-fringed lake into which the ship had suddenly dropped.

For their part, too, the two Brady kids were thoroughly fascinated by what was happening on the two sides of the moving ship. It was like watching an exciting movie and then suddenly finding themselves right in the middle of it.

For several minutes they stared hypnotically at the strong electric trains that pulled the vessel through the next lock. Only when they had successfully negotiated it and were on their way to what seemed like a river did they hear Doris Bailey's cries.

"Peter, Jan!" she yelled. "I want to talk to you." They watched her run up to them from another part of the deck and at the same moment realized with horror that Lakey and Harry were moving away. They were abandoning their shuffleboard contest entirely!

Doris Bailey, flushed and happy, rushed up to their side. "Isn't it fantastic, the canal I mean? I've never seen anything like it. All that machinery—all those people racing around doing things. I feel like there's a war going on or something. Where's Greg?"

The words tumbled out of her mouth so fast

they ran into one another. For a moment neither Jan nor Peter could comprehend her.

"Greg?" Jan said stupidly. "I don't understand. You're looking for Greg?"

"Of course. I just asked you," Doris Bailey cried impatiently. "They're starting up a big shuffleboard contest and I wanted Greg to play with me. I ran up as fast as I could to keep him from playing in this game."

"What?" Peter asked. "What are you talking about?"

Doris looked at them as if they were retarded.

"Where is he, for heaven's sake? I thought he was with you here, playing shuffleboard."

"Who told you that?" Jan asked.

"Some man. He was with another man. He walked up to me and asked if we wanted to talk to Greg and Marcia and told us about the shuffleboard games. He suggested that we form two teams. Me and Greg and Marcia and Harry."

Peter's nose began to twitch as he suspected what happened.

"What did this man look like?" he asked.

"Oh, what difference does that make?" Doris asked crossly. She looked behind him, at the retreating forms of Lakey and Harry.

"There they are. They were at Daddy and Mommy's big party the other night. They were here with you, playing shuffleboard. I saw them leave a minute ago."

Peter grabbed her arm fiercely. "Where did they go, quick."

"Down that stairway!" She pointed to a distant hatchway.

"Come on, Jan," Peter yelled. "Sorry, we gotta run!"

"Where you going?" Doris yelled after them.

"No time to talk now!" Jan replied as she tore along the deck with her brother.

"Where are we going?" she asked.

"I don't know yet," Peter answered breathlessly. "But we gotta stop them. Lakey and Harry put the Baileys on us so they could get away. They probably got Helen away from Marcia and Cindy the same way. And they're probably heading for the rich lady's cabin to rob her right now!"

"We gotta stop them!" Jan yelled, racing with him toward the hatch down which Lakey and Harry had vanished.

Chapter NINE

~~~~~~~~~~~~~~~~~~~~~~~

In another moment they had tumbled down the stairs and were speeding along the quiet, highly polished deck. There was no trace of Lakey or Harry.

"Are you sure they're on this deck, Peter?" Jan asked.

"No, I'm not sure," said Peter tersely. "I'm just guessing, but I think it's a pretty good guess. We don't know who the woman they're robbing is. But we do know she must have a lot of money. Otherwise how could she afford all that expensive jewelry, right?"

"Right!" Jan said.

"Okay, then it figures that she must be staying on this deck. This is where the most expensive suites of rooms are. I talked to one of the stewards yesterday and they call this 'Millionaires' Row' because you need a lot of money to live here. I'll be willing to bet my tape recorder against a dime that those crooks are operating right now behind one of these doors."

They walked quietly up and down the deck listening at various doors. Peter lowered his head at each keyhole to try to detect the slightest sound.

"They're in one of these cabins," Peter insisted stubbornly.

"How do you know it's *them*," Jan said. "Even if you hear a sound, couldn't it possibly be somebody who lives there?"

"No, I don't think so," Peter said. "They made a big announcement about our going through the canal last night and everybody's up there. Heck, Jan, you saw the crowds of people at the rail. They're all watching the ship go through the locks."

He stamped his foot in frustration after several minutes more of applying his ear to the doors.

"I *know* those dirty crooks are in there," he

insisted, barely controlling his fury at being helpless to do anything. "They're probably in there behind some door going through that poor woman's valises and bureaus and clothes and all. And we can't do a darn thing. If there were only some way of scaring them to death so they'd run out of there."

"Why don't we call the purser or one of the other crew members?" Jan asked helpfully.

"Because they don't believe us, Jan!" Peter told her. "We already tried that, remember? They think we're just a bunch of crazy kids making up stories. No," he said thoughtfully. "We need to surprise them in some way with something they don't expect. But what?"

Jan and he thought silently for a moment. A couple of times they looked at the other and then shook their heads no as they realized that the idea had flaws. Then suddenly Jan jumped up and down with excitement.

"Tell me," Peter begged. "What is it?"

For a moment his sister pointed speechlessly toward him. In her excitement she could not get the words out.

"What is it, Jan?" he asked impatiently.

"The tape recorder!" she finally blurted out to him.

"What about it, Jan?" he said, annoyed. "If I can't detect any sounds with my ear, I certainly can't do it with a tape recorder."

"Not *record, play,*" she said. "*Play* it."

"Play it?" he asked, puzzled.

"Of course. As loud as you can. Don't you

see what I mean? It's bound to drive them out of the cabins. No matter what they're up to."

Peter's eyes lit up finally. "Of course. They'll be hearing their own voices booming in the hall, talking about the robbery they planned. Hey, that's good thinking, Jan."

He punched her on the shoulder to show his approval. Then he turned up the volume of the machine he carried and put it close to several doors. For a moment or two nothing happened. He moved further down the deck and turned it up even louder. The hall was suddenly filled with the sounds of Oscar and Mary talking about the planned robbery—the conversation that had been recorded between the two funnels.

All of a sudden a door behind them burst open and they heard people running down the hall. As they turned to see who it was, they met the angry, incredulous eyes of Lakey, Helen, and Mary. Suddenly another door slammed on the other side.

"Get that darned recorder!" Lakey yelled at the two women. "We gotta destroy that. Get them! Don't let 'em get away."

It all happened so fast that Peter and Jan were trapped. Before they could decide which way to run to get away, they were surrounded. On one side were Lakey and the women. They saw coming at them menacingly from the other the enraged faces of Oscar and Harry.

Chapter *TEN*

~~~~~~~~~~~~~~~~~~~~~~~~~~~~~~~~~~~~

Peter and Jan struggled to get out of the crooks' clutches, but there were too many of them. When Jan tried to yell, one of the men put his hands over her mouth before any sound could come out. Another hand flew over Peter's mouth.

"Darn pesky brats!" Lakey said. "Did you get what you were looking for, Helen?"

"No," Helen said, chagrined. "I was just going through her things looking for the jewels. I think I finally found out where the old biddy hid them. Then I heard what sounded like Oscar and Mary yelling in the hall. About the robbery."

"It confused me," Mary said.

"Me too," Helen joined in. "I didn't know what was happening. I thought the whole thing had been ruined by some stewards coming through or something. Or maybe the old biddy was coming back to her room."

"You mean we've wasted all this time," Lakey said furiously. He shook Jan and Peter. "Why you dirty, stupid little runt," he cried at Peter. He pushed him vigorously, so overcome was he with rage.

"I ought to——" he began to pummel Peter,

when suddenly he howled with pain as Jan bit deeply into the back of his hand and let her teeth sink into his flesh.

"Get that stupid kid off me!" he yelled.

The others pulled Jan away but had a hard time holding the feisty girl back.

"Don't you dare touch my brother," she screamed at him. "Don't you dare touch him."

"What are you going to do with them?" Oscar said irritably. "We can't just stay here—people will be coming back."

"I'd like to push them overboard, the stinking little brats," Lakey growled. "But it would mean bringing them up on deck."

"I know what," Harry cried. "Lock them in one of the empty cabins . . . in some dark closet. Nobody'll ever find them till the next voyage. They'll starve to death."

Lakey's face broke into a smile. "You're thinking with your head Harry. Let's do it. Pick one of the empties and pitch them there—but put a gag on them first so they won't be heard by anyone coming by. They got big mouths, these two."

"Oh no, please," Mary cried. "You can't do that. They're just kids, for heaven's sake."

"Kids who want to ruin everything for all of us and get us pinched by cops in Puerto Rico," Helen sneered. "Put them in there fast I say."

"You can't do it," Mary pleaded. "They're just babies, Lakey. Have a heart. Besides, they can't prove anything. The room is undisturbed. All they could say is they saw us here. Anything else they can't prove."

"Shut up, Mary, you're getting soft in the head," Harry barked. He pushed in the door of a cabin. "Here's an empty. I'll do it myself."

"I'll help you," Lakey said. "Come on, Oscar, Helen. Give us a hand with these baboons."

He yelped in pain as Jan's teeth dug into his fingers again and her foot kicked him hard in the leg. At almost the same instant, Peter kicked Harry in the knee and stomped on Oscar's foot. For a minute the three men, jumping up and down in an effort to control their outcries of pain, let him go.

"Yell, Peter," Jan cried out. And then she began to scream for Greg and Cindy and Bobby and Marcia.

As loudly as he could, Peter shouted the same names.

"Shut them up for God's sake," Lakey screamed. "We're only a few feet below the crowds."

Oscar and Harry stared at Lakey stupidly as if they could not think what to do next. Helen began to panic visibly as the screams grew louder. Meanwhile Mary pressed her body against Jan and Peter. The hands of the men could not reach the Brady kids because Mary continued to shield them with her body. It took them several seconds to realize that she was blocking their way.

"Get away from there!" Lakey screamed at Mary.

"No," Mary screamed back, "I'm not going to let you do it!"

Lakey struck her face hard and then hurled

100

her against the opposite wall, colliding with Oscar and Harry as he did so. In the wild melee that followed, Jan and Peter ran wildly for the nearest hatch and up to the top deck.

Lakey threw his cigarette lighter against the wall in a towering rage.

"You dummy," he screeched at Mary. "You absolute dithering dummy." He slapped her hard again. "You see what they did. It's your share of the jewels you threw away too. Your share!"

Mary did not flinch under the blow. "I haven't given it up yet, Lakey. We've still got the captain's party after we land in San Juan. And we'll get much more there than we could possibly have got here." Her voice hardened. "But I warn you. You hit me once more and I'll blab this whole deal to the captain."

As she saw his face harden, she smiled. "And turn that bogeyman's face off. You can't do anything to me. You're the first one they'd look for. They'd soon find out you killed your ex-wife so you could marry little Helen here."

Lakey raised his arm. "Let's get those kids," he growled.

"Don't do it, Lakey," Mary warned. "I went into this because I need money desperately. But I am not a murderer. Let them go unless you want me to race over to the captain's cabin. We still have a good chance to get those jewels at the party and we'll get five times as much as you would here. She might have had almost

101

nothing in those bags. Why kill your big chance this way—by going after some kids?"

"Maybe you're right," Lakey said reluctantly.

Chapter ELEVEN

Up on deck, Jan and Peter breathed in deep drafts of wonderful air and sighed with relief.

"Wow," Jan said. "I thought for a minute they'd really lock us in some closet and forget us for the rest of the trip."

"Not after you nearly bit his hand off, sis," Peter said with pride. "Remind me never to get into a big argument with you. You're liable to eat off my fingers."

Jan blushed. "I don't know what happened. I got so worried they were going to hurt you and I had to do something."

Peter shook his head and grinned. "And you sure did. You and your great big beautiful teeth. You ought to give commercials for toothpaste."

"What do we do now?" she asked to change the subject, which was becoming embarrassing. She did not like to think of her teeth as big.

"Let's find Greg and Marcia, Cindy and Bobby and have another Council of War."

"Don't you think we ought to talk to the captain first?" Jan cried.

"Not before Greg. He's our leader in this thing, remember. Whatever he decides is okay with me."

A few minutes later Greg, Cindy, Marcia, and Bobby were in the girls' cabin trying to decide what to do.

"There's no point in going to the captain," Greg decided. "Like they told you, nothing's been disturbed. It would look like another wild story we made up. And they've all run off by now I'm sure."

"You mean we just let them go, like that?" Bobby asked, surprised.

"No," Greg said. "We'll nail them, don't worry. From what you overheard by the funnels, we know they'll probably try again at the party. Okay, we'll be waiting for them and when they do it, we'll catch them red-handed."

"We will?" Cindy said amazed. "How? We don't know all they're planning. We don't even know everybody on the crew that's working with them."

"That's right," Marcia said. "Maybe we'd better tell the captain the whole story and let them do it."

"And have them laugh at us again and tell us to go be nice kids? No thanks. They laughed at us once, they'll do it again. I'd rather laugh in their faces after we stop them cold ourselves. Let's take a vote okay? I'll go along with either way that's decided."

Greg paused to take breath and said: "Who's

for staying with me till we nail them down good?"

There was no sound or movement for a while. Then slowly Peter raised his hand. Then Marcia, then Jan, and finally everyone else. Greg grinned broadly, delighted by their action.

"Okay, the Brady Raiders are on the warpath," he announced proudly. "They'd better be on the alert. They'll never know what hit them."

"Very good," Jan said, laughing. "I mean that name, Brady Raiders. What made you think of it?"

"I don't know," Greg shrugged. "I guess because it fits. We're going on the attack starting today. From now on we keep tabs on them and also a steady communication with each other through signals. So if they pull anything like they did today, all of us will come running on the double to the rescue. No more being caught off base like this time."

"You mean we'll have real signals and all like Indian scouts or soldiers?" Bobby asked excitedly.

"Right!" Greg said. "Now here are the signals. If you need help, you yell 'Hey Rube'—that's an old SOS cry they use around circuses and carnivals, A guy in school whose dad works in them told me about it."

"Yeah, but we don't want them to hear us," Jan said. "That might give the whole thing away."

Greg thought for a moment. "Then whistle 'Yankee Doodle,' okay?"

"Heck, she can't whistle that," Bobby said disgustedly. "Girls can't whistle."

"I can do it better than you," Jan broke in and then proceeded to whistle it beautifully. All the kids applauded her performance.

"What if you don't want to make a sound at all," Cindy asked, frowning. "I mean if we really don't want them to know what we're doing."

"Wave a white hankie then," Greg said. "The important thing is to get help. You guys were lucky this time," he said to Peter and Jan. "You were able to break up their scheme before they did any damage. Next time it's better if we're around to help you.

"Okay guys, don't forget now. We get back to the old two-man system of watching and I want regular reports. I want to know everything they say or do and anyone new they meet. We gotta find out exactly how they plan to get the jewels at the party. Also which party. I understand from the ship's newspaper that as soon as we land in Puerto Rico, a whole series of bashes begin.

"Just remember one thing," Greg said very seriously. "We can't take anything these rats do at face value. They can change their plans overnight. Just to drive us crazy. The only way to fight them is to watch them so carefully that we can try to figure their next move."

The next two days there was nothing much to report. After the ship left the Panama Canal, it sailed through smooth, sun-dappled seas. The Caribbean, which they now entered, enchanted

105

them all with its beautiful sunsets and the magnificent splendor of the light dancing on the swells around the ship.

No matter how much they followed the crooks about the decks, they heard nothing about the coming jewel robbery. If anything, the crooks seemed more than usually silent. If they noticed their followers, they said nothing. Several times Lakey, Oscar, and Harry stared at them as if they had never seen them before. They acted as if nothing had happened. Occasionally Mary looked at them as if she wanted to say something.

Her eyes would look troubled, as if she were trying to communicate some inner distress, some information that would help them. Then she would look blank again. Whether this was because she was afraid to trust them or because she feared the vengeance of Lakey and the others, they did not know.

The strange attitude and behavior of the conspirators bothered them at first; then they forgot about it. They spent their days, when they were not on watch, swimming or playing deck tennis in the warm, golden sun. Or they would compete with Doris and Harry Bailey at shuffleboard or play dart games with Carol and Mike Brady and with Alice.

After a week of living on the ship, however, they began to wish they could set foot on land. They were happy when the vessel finally sighted Puerto Rico. The stop at the island meant excursions ashore and a chance to see the beautiful

Spanish towns and the thick rain forests of the first places in the New World visited by Columbus.

They could hardly keep still as the ship entered the incredibly beautiful Bay of San Juan with its great centuries-old Fort El Morro, fringed with waving palm trees. They knew the pirates of olden days had sailed into this harbor, that the Spaniards of the great days of discovery had set out from here to conquer Mexico and Cuba and South America and then explore Florida.

They were so eager to see the island, to visit it, that they feared Greg might force them to stay on board the ship while every one else left. Fortunately all of the crooks, including Mary, also left the vessel. Since there was no reason to stay behind, the kids eagerly chose bus tours through the picturesque island.

Greg had insisted only that they pick those buses that carried the conspirators.

"We can't let them out of our sight," he warned. "They might be meeting some new characters we should know about."

"Yes, but what about Mom and Dad and Alice," Jan asked. "Suppose they ask why we pick certain buses instead of the ones they want. We don't want to arouse their suspicions, do we?"

"I checked that already," Peter said quickly. "They said we can pick our own tours and they'll go along with us."

"Really?" Cindy said, surprised.

"Yep," Peter said. "Dad told me we had behaved so well on the ship—not starting fights or having accidents and all and he felt sorry for us because we'd been cooped up so long—well he left it up to us."

"Terriffic," Bobby said. "All we gotta do is jump on the buses the crooks take."

"Well, it's not that easy," Greg said patiently. "I mean Mom and Dad and Alice want to join us. We can't just leave them behind. What we have to do is find out which tours the crooks are taking, then divide them up among ourselves, that's all. Then we leave it up to Mom, Dad, and Alice where they want to go."

"How do we find out?" Jan asked.

"We look at the lists in the travel secretary's office near the dining room," Greg explained. "That's the lady who arranges all the shore trips on our stopovers. The passengers sign up and you can look at their names in case you have friends on a certain tour and want to join them."

"Boy, you think of everything, Greg," Marcia said.

"Just don't let them out of your sight," Greg warned. "And I want two guys on each bus the crooks take."

Chapter TWELVE

~~~~~~~~~~~~~~~~~~~~~~~~~~~~

Greg and Cindy found themselves on the bus carrying Lakey and Harry. The bus picked by the two conspirators was headed for the lovely rain forest of El Junque in the center of the island. Meanwhile it would stop briefly at various little towns en route. With them came Alice, who had never seen a rain forest before and was very curious about it.

"It's supposed to be a kind of jungle area," Alice told them, "or at least that's what the travel office lady told me. Maybe I'll meet some tall handsome man there, somebody who swings through the trees and yells 'Ooh aah! Ooh aah!' like Tarzan."

"Suppose he asks you to stay there and live in a tree house," Cindy asked, her eyes crinkling with amusement at Alice's imitation of Tarzan.

Alice's eyebrow rose at this. "Well, I think I'll climb that little tree when I come to it."

Carol and Mike Brady were on the same bus as Oscar and Mary, the bus going to the town of San Juan and its surroundings. Greg ordered the other kids to board that bus.

"What about Helen?" Marcia asked worriedly.

"Who's keeping tabs on her? She can't leave the ship with the other passengers. I spoke to the travel office lady. She says the staff get special shore leave after the passengers disembark."

"That's right," Greg said, frowning. "And we can't leave her alone. She's in too deep and she may be meeting other people working with Lakey and the rest."

He sighed. "You go with Cindy, Marcia. I'll look after Helen. After all, I arranged this whole thing."

"No, Greg, let me do it," Marcia said quickly. "It's easier for one female to follow another. It's less conspicuous. You go with Cindy and Alice and we'll report to each other when we all get back to the ship."

"Thanks, sis," he said gratefully, "you're a princess."

"I'll ask you for a favor someday, big brother," she said, grinning back at him.

Two hours later the tour buses were driving through the beautiful mountainous island.

The bus carrying Greg and Cindy and Alice moved steadily higher and higher over the mountainous roads that covered the lush countryside. Cindy was so spellbound by the sight of the pretty white houses and the farm animals that she kept turning to Greg for explanations. He told her that they were passing through sugar cane farms.

The bus driver gave a steady flow of information about their surroundings as they continued

110

through the thick cane fields. Sugar was the number-one industry in Puerto Rico, he noted, and supported many families on the island. Next was tobacco. The island also had many factories which had moved from mainland America and in which dresses and other clothes 'were made for millions of people in the United States.

"I never saw anything so mountainous as this place," Alice said. "The island's just thirty-five miles wide, they tell me, and most of it's hills and rock. I don't know how on earth they ever do their farming here. I bet every time they go plowing, they slide down one of those big hills."

A friendly Puerto Rican farmer in a wide-brimmed straw hat heard them and laughed appreciatively. "You're right, señora," he said. "It's dangerous up on those hills, especially when it's wet and the *jibaros*—that's how we call the farmers in Puerto Rico—do fall sometime."

Another Puerto Rican behind them told them how Columbus had described the island to the king of Spain after he came home from his voyage. Wanting to show the king just how hilly the new island was he picked up a sheet of paper on the table, crushed it in his hand until it was greatly wrinkled, and tossed it back before the monarch.

"That is what Puerto Rico looks like, Your Majesty," he said. The king laughed his appreciation.

Throughout the trip, Lakey and Harry watched them out of the corner of their eyes but said nothing to them. The Brady kids ignored them amid the happy conversations with the laughing, warmhearted Puerto Ricans who had joined the tour. Many of them lived in different parts of the hundred-mile-long island which belongs to the United States and wanted to see the legendary rain forest.

As for the forest, it was an experience they would never forget. On all sides of them stretched what seemed like miles of thick, green foliage. It was like being in a jungle with rain tumbling down in buckets. To walk through the narrow paths cleared for visitors, they had to wear borrowed raincoats and still their faces were drenched. But they loved the green world around them and the fierce, raucous cries of the wild birds.

They hardly noticed that Lakey and Harry had not left the bus until they got back. Greg wondered why they had come. It seemed stupid to make the trip over the mountainous roads and then not look at the forest. But he thought no more about it till they reached a small village on the way back where they stopped for a snack. When he found out, it was too late to do anything about it.

After he and Cindy and Alice had entered the restrooms, they heard the keys turn in the lock, and a second later they realized they were locked in. It had been timed perfectly. The crooks had waited for them to go inside, right after the driver's warning that he must leave in a few minutes. After locking them in, they played a loud number on the jukebox in the next room.

By the time their pounding on the doors was heard over the din of the rock music and they were let out, the bus had left. At last Greg understood why Lakey and Harry had come. It was to lure them to an out-of-the-way village and force them to remain there while they did their dirty work secretly in town. They had probably used a similar trap with Peter, Jan, Bobby, and their parents in San Juan. How on earth would they get back to town, Greg wondered. There was no bus until the next morning.

Alice frantically signaled the owner of the snack bar to try to race to where the bus was with his car and stop it. The man shook his head. The bus was already too far away. They were trapped.

Meanwhile the bus carrying Oscar and Mary through San Juan was driving through the narrow, crooked streets of the old Spanish town. At intervals, the driver would obligingly stop, point out the historic old buildings, some of them over two hundred years old, and allow the passengers to get off and see them close up. It was at one of these, near the beautiful old cathedral, that Oscar and Mary gave them the slip.

Just as the passengers were filing through the deep, high-vaulted interior of the dark church, Peter noticed that Oscar and Mary were moving toward the street door. It was obvious they were leaving the group. Peter signaled Bobby and Jan to follow him after them. Outside the two crooks ran across the street to a taxi rank, entered a car, and drove off.

"We gotta go after them," Peter said. "Quick."

"What about Mom and Dad?" Bobby interjected.

"No time," Peter blurted as he ran toward the cabs. "Greg said stay with them. We have to follow them."

A moment later their cab was following hard on the trail of Oscar's car. Full of nervous excitement, they moved along crowded streets with quaint Spanish-style houses till they reached an even more crowded community at the edge of the water. Peter wisely asked the Brady cab to stop a half block away from where Oscar and Mary alighted. They watched Oscar and Mary from their cab and in a few moments they saw the pair of conspirators meet another man who moved out of the tangle of boats docked at the end of the street. Oscar and Mary spoke to him for several minutes and then went back to their taxi. Less than an hour later they had returned to the ship. Behind them, still puzzled by the meeting with the stranger, were Peter, Jan, and Bobby.

They had no sooner mounted the gangplank than they found an anxious father and mother confronting them.

"What's going on around here anyway?" Mike yelled. "First you guys vanish and then we can't find Marcia. And what happened to Cindy and Greg? They were supposed to be back half an hour ago?"

Jan tried to soothe her parents. "Marcia's probably in the library or maybe she's visiting Doris or Harry Bailey. And Greg's bus probably just got delayed. They use a lot of very old buses here. I'm surprised some of them are still running, in fact."

"Well, if they're delayed much longer," Carol said, "Greg's going to miss the captain's gala party. It was just announced for tonight and I know Greg wanted to go very badly. He especially wanted to dance with Doris."

"Never mind the party," Mike Brady said sternly. "Where in heaven's name did you characters disappear to?"

Chapter THIRTEEN

The next few hours might have been disastrous for them all. The first thing that hit Peter, Jan, and Bobby was the awful meaning of their father's words. If Greg and Cindy were not yet back and the party was that night, they had really bungled. Their whole plan was going up in smoke. Greg was the leader, after all. Without him what chance did they have against the clever crooks?

Meanwhile they had their father's anger to

contend with. For a moment they stood there tongue-tied, unable to say anything. Finally Peter began to gurgle something.

"Well you see, Dad," he began lamely . . . "You see, we're . . . we're trying to stop . . . a . . . er . . ."

"Stop what?" Mike Brady exploded. "Unless I get some explanations soon, I'm going to withdraw all privileges. I may even keep you locked up in your cabin and bring food in on a tray. Or maybe I'll just serve you bread and water. NOW WHAT ARE YOU ALL DOING, FOR PETE'S SAKE?"

"We're trying to stop a jewel robbery, Dad," a familiar voice said behind them.

Turning in amazement they saw three dirt-streaked and exhausted travelers who looked as if they had been dragged through the mud by wild horses. Greg, Alice, and Cindy were black practically from head to toe, even their faces and their hair.

"Good grief," Mike said. "What happened to you?"

"A funny thing happened to us on the way to the ship," Alice began jokingly, making a face.

Greg explained quickly about the robbery plot, their plan to tail the crooks, and how they had been trapped in the village café. They had waited for an hour for some driver to take them into San Juan. They finally settled for seats on a horse cart carrying vegetables. A few miles from the village, they had run into a deep mud puddle. The cart had fallen on its side because of its unaccustomed load and tossed them all into the mud.

"Ugh!" cried Cindy in disgust. "I can still taste all that mud."

Suddenly they heard a burst of loud laughter.

"Hey, I love your makeup, Alice," Marcia said. "And yours too, Greg. Wait till Doris Bailey sees that. She'll go ape!"

"Never mind, Doris," Greg said, embarrassed. "What did you find out about Helen?"

"I listened at the door of a cabin on B deck when she walked into it to make a phone call," Marcia explained "right after you left this morning. I don't know who she talked to. But it sounded like someone on the crew was on the other end. She kept telling him to hurry with dinner so they could get the job done at the right moment. If they're even a little late, they may have to postpone it till the next party.

"I wish I knew who Helen talked to," she added.

"It might have been the man we saw talking to Oscar and Mary at the boat," Jan said. "They were probably letting him know the final plan for tonight's gala party."

"Tonight!" Greg shouted. "Wow! We'd better get cleaned up fast so we can get down there."

"Wait a minute, Mr. Detective," his father said grimly. "Not before we tell this all to the captain."

"Oh Dad, no, please," the kids cried out. "Please don't stop us now."

"Give us a chance, Dad," Greg begged. "We

117

don't have any hard evidence yet. The captain'll just laugh at us, like he did last time. If we go the party, we may catch them red-handed, actually trying to steal the jewels."

Mike Brady turned to his wife and saw the answer in her eyes. She didn't have the heart to stop them now, when they were close to the end of their search.

"Okay," he said. "I guess if your mother can take the pressure, so can I. But only for tonight," he added quickly.

Their faces showed their relief as he smiled.

Chapter *FOURTEEN*

By the time the conspirators showed up, the party was in full swing. The Brady kids had almost given up. They had come down early, dressed in their best clothes for the gala. First on the program was a scrumptious dinner of delicious foods they had never before tasted. And the evening was to be capped with a special dessert created for the party by the chef, music, and dancing afterwards.

Everything was going according to plan except that the crooks were not anywhere in sight. As

Greg had dictated, the kids had their eyes peeled for the familiar faces of the jewel thieves. In addition, Greg had given Peter the special responsibility of looking for the man who had met secretly with Oscar and Helen at the waterfront in San Juan.

Peter looked hard but he saw nothing. All he could see were masses of people dressed in their best finery. The women and girls all wore long dresses, the men and boys wore suits and ties. Many of the ladies wore their best jewelry as well. It was easy to tell who the richest women were. They were the ones who wore several stunning pieces at the same time: lovely pearl necklaces about their necks, large diamond rings on their fingers and diamond and emerald bracelets on their wrists. Some women even wore diamond tiaras on their heads.

The effect was breathtaking. The lights from the big chandeliers created magnificent patterns of color as they were refracted from the jewels. All of the Bradys were impressed and especially Carol, who wore only her small diamond ring.

"Look at that elderly woman over there with that diamond tiara," whispered Alice to Marcia. "It must be worth at least fifty or a hundred thousand dollars. Isn't it gorgeous?"

But Marcia was not looking. She had suddenly spotted Lakey, Helen, Oscar, and Harry coming in. A second later she caught sight of Helen. The chambermaid had come in to help with the gala party. She pretended not to see her four fellow conspirators, who sat at a table next to the one occupied by several diamond-studded ladies.

"It must be getting very close to the time," Greg whispered tensely to Peter, Marcia, Jan, Cindy, and Bobby. "Any minute now. But where's the guy we saw with them by the boats, darn it!"

They watched carefully to see what would happen next, feeling their hearts pounding furiously against their chests as the minutes ticked by. What on earth *was* the crooks' plan, they kept asking themselves, and when would it happen?

As with all good plans, it turned out to be simple. And it took them by surprise. The dinner, a great success, had just ended. Everyone had had their fill of wonderful food and wine. Now, the captain announced, the great surprise of the evening would come: crêpes suzette, delicious pancakes in a brandy sauce and brought flaming from the pans in which they were cooked to the waiting tables. And for a truly splendid effect, the captain ordered all lights out. In a second the room was plunged into darkness.

There was a hushed silence as all the diners tried to peer through the blackness. Then the captain, in his jolliest tone of voice, began counting off:

"ONE . . . TWO . . . THREE . . . at the count of ten I want the crêpes suzette to march through the room to the tune of 'Stars and Stripes Forever.' "

It was a magnificent idea and it would have stunned them all if something much more startling and totally unexpected had not intervened. In the midst of the captain's counting, a woman's scream pierced the darkness. "I've been robbed!" she yelled.

Almost at once more shrieks followed as other women yelled that they too had been robbed of their jewels. Then everything happened. People started screaming at one another, someone yelled for the lights, and someone else overturned a table. For several minutes there was sheer bedlam.

All at once the lights came back on. While still blinking, Peter saw the man who had met Oscar near the boats. He was in a steward's uniform and he was carrying a bundle of used napkins toward Helen, who was watching him nervously from her post on the other side of the large room.

"Hey, that's the guy who was with Oscar," Peter yelled to Greg. The man, who had heard Peter, broke into a run toward Helen.

"Let's go after him," Greg shouted. Immediately the other Brady kids leaped from their table and ran after him. Mike and Carol jumped up and tried to stop them but failed. "What are those kids up to?" Mike said, annoyed.

Seeing his pursuers draw close, the steward rolled up his napkins into a ball and threw it to Helen, who was approaching from the other side. The bundle missed because another steward ran between them with a tray of crêpes.

121

As the bundle hit the floor, Peter, the steward, and Helen all scrambled for it.

"Don't let them get it!" Greg yelled to Jan, Bobby, Marcia, and Cindy. "It's probably got the jewels in it."

In a flash several bodies were tumbling on the floor, grasping desperately at the bundle. Marcia had just got her hands on it when Helen stepped on her fingers. In the ensuing tangle, the steward managed to seize the bundle, jumped up with it, and ran. The room was still such a madhouse of people running and yelling that no one noticed him except the Brady kids.

"After him kids, quick!" Greg yelled. In another instant, all six of the Brady Bunch were in hot pursuit of the steward. The man leaped into the nearest corridor and then down a stairway leading to the deck with the swimming pool. The kids raced right after him, startling everyone in the big dining hall. The captain stared at them dumbfounded.

In the vast pool chamber, the steward ran around the pool rim, several yards ahead of the Bradys. A single, solitary swimmer in the water stopped and stared at them.

"Go around the other side," Greg ordered Peter and Jan. "We'll box him in so he can't get away."

Obeying orders, Peter and Jan ran the other way and in a moment had the steward surrounded. The steward stared at them helplessly and then stunned them by leaping into the pool.

At the same moment the swimmer dived under the surface.

Greg waved to Peter and Marcia and they all three jumped in after the steward. For a moment they could make out nothing in the green water, then they saw the steward reaching out with his bundle to the swimmer, who tried to wrest it from his hand.

Before the swimmer could reach the bundle, Peter grabbed his legs and Marcia dove between him and the steward. Greg took this opportunity to seize the bundle. Then he swam away with furious strokes. When he got to the rim, the two crooks grabbed at his legs but with Peter and Marcia diving under and biting their legs they had to let go.

Greg jumped up on the rim and threw the bundle to Jan, who gave it to Cindy. Cindy and Bobby ran toward the entrance of the pool chamber and almost collided with the captain and several members of the crew. In another moment it was all over. The ship's officers grabbed the two thieves and forced them to remain with their face to the wall. Then they checked the bundle. It was filled with jewels: bracelets, necklaces, brooches, and pins—a fortune's worth.

The captain stared at the rich haul as if he could not believe it.

"I think you owe these children an apology, Captain," a familiar voice said behind them. They turned to see Mike and Carol Brady and Alice.

"I think you're right," the captain said. "I'm

sorry, children. I should have taken you more seriously."

"You'd better get those guys in the dining room," Greg said. "Before they get away! Including their friends."

The captain nodded and, moving to a telephone on the wall, gave orders that Oscar, Lakey, and Harry be arrested and that no one be allowed to leave the ship.

"You can point out their other helpers to us as soon as we go upstairs," the captain said quietly.

"I'd like to make one request, sir," Peter said.

The captain nodded. "What is it?"

"There's a woman named Mary among them. She saved us from being badly hurt. Could you go easy on her please?"

"Of course," the captain said. "I'll do everything possible. But isn't there anything you'd like for yourselves? I mean you'll probably get a reward from all the grateful ladies whose jewels you saved. But surely there is something I can do to make up for my own shortsightedness."

Greg looked at his brothers and sisters and then at Mike and Carol and Alice, who were eyeing them with great pride. He motioned to the other kids to come closer for a huddle. For a moment they spoke in whispers. Finally, grinning, he turned to the captain.

"Well, there is something," he said shyly. "Could you let us steer the ship some time?"

The captain and the purser stared at one another for a moment and then the captain smiled.

"Why not? Come up anytime you like. All of you. Judging from the way you managed this thing, you can probably handle the wheel as well as anyone on this ship."